D1827484

LET IT KILL YOU

ANDY RAUSCH

Copyright (C) 2019 Andy Rausch

Layout design and Copyright (C) 2019 by Next Chapter

Published 2019 by Terminal Velocity – A Next Chapter Imprint

Cover art by Cover Mint

This book is a work of fiction. Names, characters, places, and incidents are the product of the author's imagination or are used fictitiously. Any resemblance to actual events, locales, or persons, living or dead, is purely coincidental.

All rights reserved. No part of this book may be reproduced or transmitted in any form or by any means, electronic or mechanical, including photocopying, recording, or by any information storage and retrieval system, without the author's permission.

For Kristin with love

Find what you love and let it kill you.

CHARLES BUKOWSKI

ACT ONE

PROLOGUE

MANNY'S EYES were as big as silver dollars as he looked at Chino Genetti, holding a .45 in his face. *"Please, no,"* begged Manny. *"Please don't kill me."*

"Why would I let you live?" asked Chino.

"I ain't so bad, man. I'm a good guy. Sure, I done killed a buncha motherfuckers and sold smack, but I'm a good guy, deep down."

Chino's phone went off. Chino looked at Manny, gun still in his face, and reached for the phone. "Hold on, I got a text," he said. Chino looked at his phone, seeing the text was from Dobbs. It read: I'M AT GRILLBY'S. WHERE U AT?

Chino looked at Manny. "Sorry. This'll just

take a second." Chino held up the phone, hit a button, and spoke into it. "Running late. I'm at work. Be there soon." He stopped and looked at the phone, reading his message back. He looked at Manny, shaking his head.

"Fuckin' speech to text," he said. "You heard what I said, right? But speech to text thinks I said, 'Running laid. I'm a jerk.' You believe that?" He looked back down, continuing. "'Beater spoon.'" He looked at Manny. "*'Beater spoon'?* What does that even mean?" Looking into Manny's frightened eyes, he said, "I don't know why I use this feature. It takes me longer to fix the fuckin' message than it would to just type it. But I got fat fingers and I don't like to type."

Manny was looking at him crazy. *"What the fuck, man?"*

Chino considered fixing the message but decided to wait. He stuck the phone back in his pocket.

"What can I do to stop this?" asked Manny, frantic now. "I got money. You want money? I can pay."

"You wanna hear a joke?" Chino asked.

"What?"

"Knock knock."

Manny stared at him, trying to understand.

Chino straightened the pistol, trying to intimidate him. “You say 'Who's there?' Let's try again.”

Manny stared at him.

“Knock knock.”

“Okay. Who's there?”

Chino squeezed the trigger, firing a round into Manny's face, dropping him. Standing there staring at the body, he considered messaging Dobbs. No, he would wait. He still had to do the thing with the ice picks.

ONE

Chino had just killed Manny, and now Dobbs was giving him shit about being a mediocre hitter. "Listen, white boy, you don't know how to kill a motherfucker properly." Of course this was bullshit. Chino was the most feared hitter in the city, but he let him have his fun and tell his jokes. And that's what they were—*jokes*. Dobbs, a decade older than Chino, had been a hitter once, too. This was back before Cocoa had taken over. Dobbs had been a good, solid hitman. But he wasn't on Chino's level. It was the difference between a career .280 hitter and Ted Williams. They both played the game, and they both played well, but they weren't close to being the same.

Since Dobbs had retired, he'd spent his days drinking, chasing tail, and talking shit. They joked around and gave each other hell—Dobbs calling him an amateur, and Chino making jokes about Dobbs being an old man. But Chino and Dobbs were best friends. In fact, Dobbs was the only person Chino considered a friend at all. He'd walked away from everyone else after his wife and kids had been killed.

Scratch that. Chino had *two* friends—Dobbs, and Jack Daniels.

Chino knew Dobbs cared and that their relationship ran deeper than jokes because Dobbs incessantly griped about his alcoholism. "That shit's gonna kill you faster than bitches or bullets," he always said. It wasn't like Chino didn't know; he just didn't care. Since he'd lost Aliesha, Tyrese, and Kailee, he'd lost his will to live. Now he functioned on autopilot. He was alive, but that was a technicality. That was what the world saw—a living, breathing human. But the reality was, Chino was as dead as his family.

Chino drank. And when he drank, he drank beyond excess. He didn't know if it would be the whiskey or a bullet that would inevitably kill him, but he was ready either way.

Dobbs was still talking shit. "You're a terrible hitter, Cheen."

"You think I'm a shitty hitman? Take it up with my mentor. I learned it from him, so he musta been shitty, too."

"Nah. I hear Dobbs was a world-class hitter back in the day."

"Oh, do you? This 'back in the day', when was this? Before TV? Back when there were dinosaurs and shit?"

"You sayin' I'm old, motherfucker?"

"I'm sayin' your ass was there when they invented dirt."

"You think you're funny, but you ain't. That's why you never made it as a comic."

This was another thing Dobbs gave him hell for. When Chino had been in his early twenties, he'd worked as a stand-up comic. But he'd failed, as most comics do. Once, when he'd performed at The Comedy Cellar, Colin Quinn told him, "Ninety-six percent of comics fail. Think about that. If you went in for a surgery and the doctor told you ninety-six percent of the patients who had that surgery died, you wouldn't go through with it." And Chino ultimately became part of the ninety-six percent. He hadn't been the best comic, but he wasn't a bad one either. Just mediocre. He'd had his share of nights when the crowd laughed at every joke, just as he'd had plenty of nights when he'd been booed and heckled.

Chino was never ashamed of failing though. Because of his failure, he'd then found the one thing he was genuinely good at—killing people. This wasn't the kind of thing he could put on his resume' or brag about, but he didn't need to. When you were as good a hitter as Chino was, people *knew*. Chino was afforded a level of respect in the crime world that very few people got, and he'd earned it. He'd paid his dues and he'd done his job well. You want proof? Just ask any of the sixty-four people Chino had put in the ground. Except you can't, cause they're all dead.

Chino had first gone to work for Cocoa back in 1998, when he was twenty-five. He'd already worked as a knockaround guy for Sonny Debrezio and had made a name for himself as a standup guy. Then he'd started training under Dobbs to become a hitter. After Sonny Debrezio died and Cocoa took over, she reached out to Dobbs to come work for her. Dobbs did for a bit, but he ultimately stepped down. Chino then went to work in his place. Nobody had been all that sure about him at first. He was new and fresh-faced, and his cocky attitude made people skeptical. But that skepticism soon subsided after

Chino had his first ten or twelve notches on his belt.

Chino had always had a solid relationship with Cocoa. They respected one another, and truth be told, Chino had always found her extremely attractive for an older woman. But now, Chino being forty-six himself, he realized she hadn't been all that old. She was eleven years older than he was, making her fifty-seven now, and she was still as fine a woman as God had ever made. But she was attractive like a siren. She was drop-dead gorgeous, yes, but ten times as dangerous. In her two decades as boss, she had proven time and time again that she was more than willing to kill anyone who crossed her. And this was good for Chino, as it had given him steady work.

Chino and Cocoa had slept together once, back in the beginning. She'd entertained him at her place, and they'd had a few drinks. This was before he'd married Aliesha, but they had been dating. Chino had never been particularly proud of this. Mostly because he'd cheated on Aliesha, but also because he could have ruined his career and ended his life by doing so. But both Chino and Cocoa had a good time that night, and neither of them ever spoke of it again. Cocoa would sometimes flirt with him, but Chino had learned over the years that she flirted with lots of guys.

Today's mark, Chino's sixty-fourth, had been a Puerto Rican drug dealer named Manny Dominguez. Manny, like a lot of young bucks with newfound money and power, had gotten cocky and overstepped his boundaries. Cocoa had overlooked these *faux pas* for a while, until Manny blatantly disrespected her, calling her a black bitch. Cocoa then sent Chino to pay him a visit.

"Tell me about Manny Dominguez," said Dobbs.

"You mean the *late* Manny Dominguez."

Dobbs chuckled. "That's the one. Tell me about 'im."

"Not much to say, really. I went over to his place, gaudy-ass apartment with pink neon lights on the walls..."

"Puerto Ricans love that gaudy shit."

"Fuckin' guy had Elvis all over the place. Posters and gold records, you know. He had Elvis plates on the walls and Elvis statues on the tables. Elvis shit *everywhere*. It looked like Graceland had gone over there and thrown up all over the place."

"Lots of Elvis."

"Man, this dude had more Elvis shit in his apartment than the whole city of Memphis got. I bet Manny had more pictures of Elvis than Elvis' mama had."

"I ain't never seen a Puerto Rican loved Elvis."

"Well, now Manny can meet the motherfucker face-to-face."

Dobbs burst into laughter. "Maybe I was wrong. Maybe you are funny."

"Of course I'm funny, jackass."

Chino took a drink, and Dobbs looked at him, serious now. "How's the job?"

Chino shrugged. "The job is the job. It don't change."

"How about Cocoa? Things good with her?"

"I can't complain."

"Wouldn't nobody listen anyway."

"She treats me good, but I'm gettin' tired."

"Of the life?"

Chino nodded. "You know how it is. Shit gets old."

"That's why I quit."

"I feel like I do the same thing every day. It's like I'm trapped in *Groundhog Day*, only instead of Bill Murray savin' people, my ass is killin' 'em."

"But you get paid *well* for that shit."

"That didn't stop you from leavin'."

"That's true. But I didn't make as much money as you."

"Would it have changed your mind if you had?"

"Nah."

"You miss it though," said Chino. "I see it on your face and I hear it in your voice. That's why you ask me about it."

"You don't know shit."

"You know I'm right, old man."

"I miss it a little, I guess. But I don't miss getting' my ass shot at, and I don't miss dealin' with asshole bosses."

"Sonny Debrezio was a piece of work."

"*All* of 'em. You really think Cocoa is different? 'Cause I got news for ya, Cheen. She ain't. At the end of the day, all them motherfuckers are the same. They're all out for numero uno. Every single one. It's all about the Benjamins. If it don't make dollars, it don't make sense. You stay around long enough, her need for you is gonna run out. Then where you gonna be?"

Chino took a drink and looked at him. "I dunno."

"At the bottom of the Hudson. That's where."

Chino saw the truth in Dobbs' words. The crime world was the best job there was when things were good, but it rarely ended well. You usually ended up dead or in prison. Chino didn't care about dying, but he didn't wanna go to prison.

"You gonna retire?" asked Dobbs.

"It's just somethin' I'm kickin' around."

"But you're considerin' it."

"Yeah, but I don't know what I would do if I wasn't killin'."

"Your ass would drink."

"I already do that."

"You're damn right you do. You're drinkin' yourself into the ground. But if you quit, you'll drink more, and you'll get there faster."

"So what exactly are you tellin' me? You're tellin' me to quit or I'll die, but then you say if I quit I'll die faster. So what are you saying?"

Dobbs turned his head, considering it. Then he turned back, looking at him. "The hell if I know. I always been full of shit. You know that."

"I never met a motherfucker was more fulla shit."

"How about Jimmy Cap? You remember him? That was a motherfucker fulla shit all day long."

"He was," said Chino, nodding. "But guess what? You got him beat. You're the king of bein' fulla shit."

"That's prob'ly right."

"I'm *always* right."

"Motherfucker, you ain't never right. Even a stopped clock is right twice a day, but not you. But if you wanna *think* you're right, you go ahead and think it. It'll just be one more thing you're wrong about."

TWO

It was just after nine, and Chino had already hit the snooze button a half dozen times before Domino called. Chino grabbed the phone and looked at it through slitted eyes. "Christ," he muttered. Had it been literally anyone else, he would have ignored it and gone back to sleep. But he couldn't skip this call. Domino was Cocoa's right-hand man, and when the boss calls, you answer.

"Yeah?"

"Cocoa wants you to come in."

This was unexpected since he'd just killed Manny the night before. His jobs were usually spaced out weeks or months apart. "She got a job for me?"

"Well, she ain't inviting you over to watch Kubrick movies."

"I'm shocked, Dom."

"'Bout what?"

"I wouldn'ta guessed you were a Kubrick guy."

"Why's that?"

"I figured you were too stupid for highbrow stuff. I woulda pegged you as a Michael Bay guy."

Chino grinned, waiting to hear Domino tell him to go fuck himself. But Domino just hung up. The dumb bastard was learning.

Chino climbed out of bed, completely naked, and strolled through the house. He fixed himself a drink and took his vitamins. Then he switched on the stereo and played some Biggie as he took a shower, shaved, and got dressed. He was ready to go a half hour after speaking to Dom. He took one last drink, locked up, and left.

Traffic was light, and it took him twenty minutes to get to Cocoa's place in Brooklyn Heights. He parked the Beamer and walked towards the two guards standing outside. He knew them both, Eddie and Dink, and nodded as he strolled past into the building. He took the elevator up to the penthouse. When he got off, he was met by Cocoa's bodyguard, Dameon. Chino liked Dameon but didn't know him well. He believed they respected one another but couldn't be sure. Maybe all the admiration was on his end. Dameon had once been a fullback for the Buccaneers but had ended his career after a string of injuries. The guy was younger than Chino, probably about thirty-two, and he was solid muscle.

"What's up, my dude?" asked Dameon.

"Not a fuckin' thing."

Dameon nodded and knocked on the door. Chino watched as the peephole darkened. A moment later, the door opened and Dameon stepped aside. Chino strode in and was met by punk-ass Domino. Domino was a big sumo-looking Puerto Rican with a bad attitude and an IQ too low for a midget to limbo under. The guy had worked for Cocoa for a few years, and Chino never understood why she employed him. There were some guys Chino could take one look at and know with certainty he could take in a fight. Domino was one of those. Chino hated the fucker, even though he couldn't pinpoint why, and the feeling was mutual. They were in a perpetual pissing match, sneering and grinning at one other, exchanging snide remarks. Cocoa rarely said anything, and Chino thought it was either because it amused her or because Domino annoyed her, too, and she liked seeing somebody giving him a hard time.

"I got a question, Dom," Chino said. "Which do you do more, eat cheeseburgers or lift weights?"

"What do you mean?"

"It means you look like you do too much of both. You look like you could bench press a Cadillac, but you also look like you just ate one."

Domino stood there trying to look tough. "And you ain't shit."

"Yeah?" asked Chino. "If you and me got in a fight, we both know how it would end. I'll give you a spoiler, kid—you'd be on the floor pickin' up your goddamn teeth."

Domino grinned. "You think so?"

"I *know* so. There are some things in life that you can't dispute. Water is wet, the sun is bright, and you're a sorry sack of shit."

Domino tried to buck up, getting in Chino's face. They were nose to nose now, and Chino didn't back down.

"Why don't you say that to my face?"

"Why don't you suck my dick?"

Domino just stood there, looking dumb. He'd painted himself into a corner and he knew it. Chino had called his bluff, and Domino couldn't do a thing about it. Chino knew Domino would tell himself he didn't do anything because Cocoa wouldn't allow it, but they both knew that was bullshit.

Chino doubled down. "Fix me a drink, bitch."

Domino was seething. He was trying to figure out what to do when Cocoa, sitting on the couch behind, said, "Do what Chino says and get him a drink."

Chino smirked. "Whiskey. Rocks."

Domino stalked away, a scowl plastered on his face. Chino looked up at Cocoa, sitting there looking sexy as hell. The woman never aged, and if she did, it was like a fine wine. She was sprawled out, wearing a skimpy black skirt, with her long, taut legs fully extended. Chino tried not to stare at them, although he wanted to; especially those pretty feet with the painted toenails and toe rings.

He looked at her, keeping his eyes locked on hers. "What's up?"

She smiled a seductive smile, but then she always smiled seductively. Everything she did was seductive. She was the type of woman that could get a motherfucker in trouble real quick, and Chino constantly reminded himself to steer clear of her traps. One wrong move, and he could end up lying next to Manny in a hole somewhere. She motioned towards a chair. "Have a seat."

He nodded and sat down.

"You lookin' good, Chino."

"Thanks."

"Everything go okay last night?"

"Motherfucker's dead. Not much else to say."

"And you did what I asked? Stuck ice picks in both his eyes?"

"Plus put a bullet in his face."

"Get much resistance?"

"I had to kill a few guys. Nothin' serious."

"I wouldn't think so."

He smiled. "I should charge extra for goons and lackeys."

"What would be fair, about a dollar apiece?"

"That's too much. These nickel and dime motherfuckers ain't worth half that."

"You're a good hitter, Chino. Nobody can say otherwise." She looked towards the kitchen, where Domino had disappeared. "I don't think Domino cares for you."

Chino smirked. "You don't say."

"Why you always fuckin' with him, Chino? He's not *that* bad."

Chino gave her a sarcastic look. "Guy looks like he went to Sizzler and wiped out the whole buffet. And he's got the intelligence of a retarded infant. And his demeanor..."

She stopped him. "He's my *consigliere.*"

"Sorry. Just stating facts we both know."

She nodded and grinned. "You're funny, Chino." She looked back towards the kitchen, seeing Domino reemerge. She leaned towards Chino and whispered, "I wouldn't drink that if I was you."

Chino smiled, turning towards Domino. Domino handed him the glass.

"You spit in this?" asked Chino.

Domino shrugged. "Maybe worse."

Chino looked him in his eyes. "You didn't."

"You don't think?"

"No. Because I scare you, and you don't want me to hurt you."

Domino started to respond, but Chino turned back towards Cocoa, ignoring him. She looked at Domino, waving him away. Domino frowned and sulked his way to the corner.

Chino sat there staring at his drink.

Cocoa chuckled. "You gonna drink it?"

"Fuck no. Dumb motherfucker probably jerked off in it."

She laughed. "Nobody makes me laugh like you, Chino."

He sat the drink on the glass table beside

him. "Aside from makin' you laugh, why am I here?"

"I got another job."

"That's quick."

"I got a bitch needs clipped."

"A *bitch*? As in a *woman*?" He turned back towards Domino. "Or you mean a man-bitch like him?"

Cocoa didn't smile. "It's a woman."

"No offense, but you know my rule—no women."

"Maybe you got too many rules."

"I only got one, and it's not new."

Cocoa looked at him, still smiling, but somehow menacingly serious. "Haven't I always done right by you, Chino?"

"I'm not saying—"

"Answer the question. *Haven't I*?"

He nodded.

"Then do me this solid and I'll never ask again."

Chino sat there, flustered. He didn't wanna do this. He believed if he did it once, he'd be expected to do it again. He hated that she put him in this position. He'd always felt close to her and had always sought to please her. It was more than just attraction. There was something about her; something he couldn't define. And she had, as she'd said, treated him well.

"Who is it?"

"Does it matter?"

"Humor me."

"No one important," she said. "Just a regular ol' bitch. Nightclub singer. Probably wants to be Rhianna."

"Why her?"

"She's not the problem," said Cocoa. "It's her dipshit daddy."

"Who's her daddy?"

"It don't matter, Chino. I need to teach him a lesson."

"By capping his kid?"

She nodded. "If that don't teach him, nothin' will. Let's get to it. You gonna do it?"

Chino sat there thinking, disappointed with himself because he knew he was gonna say yes. He nodded. "Just this once."

"Good. You do this for me and I'll make it up to you." She said it in a seductive way, maybe hinting she'd sleep with him if he did the thing. She gave him a hard-on for sure, but he would never screw her again.

Cocoa turned towards Domino. "Get the file."

Domino nodded and disappeared into the

next room. While he was gone, Cocoa made small talk. "How's the killin' game?"

"Same old same. Pays the bills."

Cocoa smiled, taking a drink from a mug that said WORLD'S BEST BOSS. Domino returned with a folder, making a point of giving him the stink eye as he handed it to him. "How quickly you need this done?" asked Chino.

"I'd like her in the ground by the end of the week."

THREE

Chino still hadn't opened the folder when he went to the bar that afternoon. He made his way through the smoky establishment. Smoking in bars had been illegal for years, but Grillby's had a strict "who gives a fuck?" policy. Chino approached the bar, glancing over at Dobbs sitting in the corner. When the bartender, Arno, came over, he said, "The normal?" Chino nodded. As Arno prepared his drink, he said, "How's the weather in your world?" Chino shrugged. "Dark and rainy, as usual." Arno chuckled and said, "Ain't that the fuckin' truth?" He gave him his drink and Chino took it, making his way over to Dobbs.

There was some bluesy guitar number on the

jukebox that Chino didn't know. He sat down beside Dobbs who was reading the *Post*.

"What's news?"

Dobbs looked up. "Nothin' good *ever*. I don't even know why I bother readin' the shit. Life is depressing enough without goin' and findin' more shit to depress me. How 'bout you?"

"Busy day already. Got called in to see the woman."

"Cocoa?"

Chino gave him a sarcastic look. "Nah. Michelle Obama."

"I thought maybe you'd gone and found you a woman."

Chino chuckled. "Those days are over for me, pal."

"Not for me."

Chino took a drink, looking over the edge of his glass.

Dobbs said, "I picked up a woman last night was hot as a firecracker. Pretty face, pretty ass, the whole nine."

"You get laid?"

"Nah, man, we made a connection. Sometimes you ain't gotta have sex for it to be good."

"Wouldn't give it up, huh?"

Dobbs shrugged. "Nah, but we goin' out again tomorrow."

"She's into you then?"

"Man," said Dobbs. "All of 'em are into me. You know that. You've met me."

"I have. That's why I was shocked."

Dobbs looked at him sideways. "What the hell you know? I been knockin' boots since before you was born."

"Your ass was ten when I was born."

"What can I say? I got an early start."

Chino stared at him. "You got started at ten?"

"Sure."

"With who?"

"You betta ask ya mama 'bout that, son."

They both chuckled.

"What did Cocoa want?" asked Dobbs.

"Another job."

"*Damn.* You just popped Manny yesterday, and you already got more work? No rest for the wicked, huh?"

"Job security. As long as the bodies keep fallin', the money keeps stackin'. So I'm good."

"True," said Dobbs, nodding. "Who you got this time?"

"I didn't want this one."

"What makes it different?"

"It's a woman."

Dobbs looked him in the eyes. "Why's that a

big thing? I killed a couple. Wasn't nothin' personal. Part of the job."

"You didn't feel bad about it?"

"No worse than I did cappin' anybody else. Shit wasn't fun with anybody. But at the end of the day, it was the same. It wasn't like I knew 'em. I just showed up, did my thing, went home and watched the Knicks."

"I said I'd never do it," said Chino.

"But you gonna do it now?"

"Yeah, but I told her I wasn't gonna do anymore."

Dobbs looked startled. *"Anymore jobs?"*

"No. No more *women*. But I don't really wanna do many more jobs either. Like I said, I'm tired of this. I'm ready for somethin' different."

"You got any money saved? It ain't like you can go back to doin' comedy. If you wasn't funny when you was twenty-two, your ass ain't gonna be funnier at forty-five."

"Forty-six," Chino corrected.

"You say that like there's a difference."

"That's true. Everything after forty is the same."

"Just wait till your ass turns fifty. Then you'll think forty was young."

"Forty ain't young. Forty is old. It's just that fifty is older."

"You know what they say."

"What's that?"

"Fifty is the new thirty."

Chino laughed. "That's bullshit. They say everything is the new somethin', no matter how old you are. Eighty is the new sixty. 'Cept it ain't. You know why? Because you might convince yourself you're younger, and you might even convince other people, but you can't convince God. He's still gonna know, and when he's ready for your ass, he's comin' no matter what. You try tellin' him that shit. 'Eighty is the new sixty.' He'll look at you like 'man, please. You're comin' with me, you old bastard.'"

Dobbs laughed. "Maybe you're funnier than I give you credit for." They both laughed and Dobbs added, "But only marginally funnier. Like, you're funnier than I thought you were, but you still ain't funny."

"Thanks."

"I wouldn't want you gettin' a swollen head. You got a fat-ass head to begin with."

"What would I do without you, Dobbs?"

"You'd be a sad, lonely motherfucker, I'll tell you that."

"Nah. I'd be alright."

"But really, you got any money saved back?"

"Not much. I got some, but not enough to last."

"Then I guess you best keep workin'."

Chino nodded. "I guess so."

"You know what your problem is, Cheen?"

"No, but I'm sure you're gonna tell me."

"The problem is, you think it's sexist to kill a woman. But I'm callin' bullshit on that. It ain't sexist at all. In fact, it's the opposite. Women wanna be treated like equals, so bustin' a cap in a broad is the same as bustin' a cap in anybody else. Ain't no difference at all 'cept she ain't got no dick. Besides, if Cocoa wants her dead, she probably did somethin' to deserve it."

"Therein lies the problem."

"There's a problem?"

"Cocoa says she didn't do anything."

Dobbs looked surprised. "So what's up?"

"Apparently this is about her daddy. Cocoa wants to teach him a lesson."

Dobbs nodded. "One of them deals. Okay. But you know, it ain't none of your business, Cheen. This is what you do—you kill people. Like in the Marines, 'we kill 'em and let God sort 'em out.'"

"I suppose you're right."

. . .

That night when Chino got home, he put Tribe Called Quest on the turntable and sat in his recliner to have a drink. He picked up the folder. He opened it and saw a one-page file and two black-and-white photos.

The mark's name was Ericka Green. It listed her name, age (she was forty), and address. There was a brief two paragraph bio saying she sang on weekends at a club called Henry's in the Bronx. It also listed a couple of her friends and family members.

Then he turned to the photos. The moment he saw Ericka Green, he felt an immediate reaction. It wasn't a physical one, really, so much as it was an emotional one. The light-skinned black woman was pretty—more than pretty, gorgeous really—but in a normal, everyday kind of way. She wasn't the lead actress in the movie, but more like the lead actress' best friend. She was attractive—right in Chino's wheelhouse—but she wasn't gonna be offered a truckload of money to do some big modeling gig. But there was something about her. Something unmistakable. *Je Ne Sais Quoi*.

The photos made him feel something in his heart and soul. It wasn't a sexual thing. It was more of a yearning to meet her. To be around her. To know her. He'd heard people say love at first sight didn't exist, but he knew otherwise. When he'd first met Aliesha, he'd taken one look at her and he'd known instantly.

Chino felt sad for Ericka Green. But even more, he felt bad for himself. But no matter how you sliced it, she had to die.

FOUR

Henry's Place was a cool club, the kind of place Chino would have enjoyed twenty years earlier. Back when he actually enjoyed going places and seeing people he wasn't paid to kill. It was a nice, smoky dive bar (was anyone paying attention to the no smoking law these days?), dark and filled with ambiance. It was a Friday night, and it was fairly full. Most of the crowd was black, but there were some white folks here too, a mixture of bohemian hippie wannabes and bearded, cooler-than-thou hipsters. The place had a relaxed atmosphere. It was still early, just after seven, and there wasn't a band playing. There were drums onstage and a piano to the left, but no one to man them. There was just some kind of laid back jazz fusion stuff that Chino liked but didn't know, playing over the speakers.

Chino ordered a drink and then found a seat near the back. As he sat, he watched the crowd, speaking to one another, oblivious to him. Maybe it was creepy, but Chino enjoyed people-watching and had developed a rather keen ability to read people, even at a distant, passing glance. For instance, there was a couple at the next table, a laid back black guy, probably upper twenties with a younger, hyperactive blonde chick. Their appearances—attitude, clothing, energy—didn't seem to match at all, and Chino figured they wouldn't last.

Chino's eyes scanned the crowd, falling on the pervy-looking older dude who looked out of place. The guy was dressed like the straightest-laced, most boring fucker ever, and he was at least a decade older than the second oldest person here. Chino wasn't young, but he was probably three decades younger than this guy. Looking at him, Chino concluded this was a guy who banged hookers. Probably super young ones. But this was New York City, and it was filled with a wide variety of weirdos, each with their own crazy fashion and fetish.

He spotted a ridiculously-attractive black

woman standing by the bar. She hadn't been there when he'd come in. Staring at her, standing there in her slinky black dress, he recognized her. It was Ericka Green. His eyes locked on her from across the room, Chino was even more convinced he could love her. But could she love him? That was the $64,000 question, wasn't it? Not that it mattered since she was gonna die. He wasn't here to kill her tonight, but eventually he would. He could do it tonight, sure, but he wanted to check out her act, see what she was all about.

He didn't know why he was waiting. At least that's what he told himself. But deep down, he knew the reason but refused to acknowledge it. After all, he was Chino Genetti, the most feared contract killer on the East Coast. He was far too professional to allow personal feelings to cloud his judgment.

And yet here he was, watching her, waiting for her to go onstage. Sparing her life. If this wasn't his judgment being clouded, then what was? The thought was present in his mind, as impossible to miss as an elephant in the room, but he tamped it down, trying his damnedest to avoid it. No, he would just drink his drinks and listen to her sing. That would be it.

He thought of Aliesha. He thought of the

kids, too, but mostly he thought of Aliesha. Because of Ericka Green. It wasn't even Ericka Green so much as what she represented. Because looking at her, he concluded that he was still capable of love. He had given up hope of ever being in love again, but now he knew it was possible. It wouldn't be Ericka Green, but it could be *someone*.

He took a drink and told himself not to overthink things. But looking at Ericka Green, there was no need to overthink. He could see everything he'd ever loved and appreciated in a woman. It went beyond her appearance, although that resonated, as well. He couldn't have put a finger on it if pressed, but he *knew*—or at least believed he did—that she was special; that she was the kind of woman he could love and adore. It was like she had an aura radiating from her that told him she was everything he believed a woman should be. But again, none of this mattered. She would be dead soon.

After watching her standing at the bar talking with people for a good half hour, an emcee finally stepped onstage. He was a nicely-dressed black man who was roughly Chino's age. "I wanna welcome everybody back tonight," the man said. "I hope you're all havin' a good time." He looked off the stage towards a man sitting near the front. "How about you, my man?" The man responded, but Chino couldn't hear the response. "Great," said the emcee. "I'm happy to hear that, brother." He then looked back out at the rest of the crowd. "As you guys know, we've got a special performer with us tonight. But she's here a lot. She's the reason most of you came out tonight." He smiled a big grin, looking over at Ericka, who was stepping onstage. "I know she's the reason I came here tonight.". There were chuckles around the room. "Ladies and gentlemen, give a warm round of applause for our own Miss Ericka Green."

The room clapped heartily and Ericka took the mic. The emcee walked off the stage. Ericka looked up, Light caught her eyes, and there was a glint. A beautiful, perfect glint. Chino felt a chill run down his spine, and he was sure he felt his heart fluttering the same flutter it had when he'd met Aliesha.

"Hello everybody," she said, her voice sweet and silky. "How you guys feelin' tonight? My name is Ericka Green. Tonight I'd like to sing you a few songs, if that's okay with you." She smiled a gorgeous, perfect smile, and some guy to Chino's left whistled. She looked in the man's direction, saying, "You're so sweet. I want to start tonight with a classic. Do you guys know Nat

King Cole?" There were claps around the room, and Chino wondered how many of these people were actually familiar with Nat King Cole. "This is a song he made famous," she said. She looked to her left, looking at a Hispanic woman now sitting at the piano. The woman started to play softly.

"Normally this song is done with strings," said Ericka. "But tonight we're gonna do it with just my friend Nicole on piano. I hope you like it." And then she started her rendition of "When I Fall in Love."

It was at this moment Chino himself fell head over heels in love.

FIVE

After Ericka had sung seven or eight songs, she wrapped up her set and thanked everyone for coming out. The emcee returned and asked everyone to give her a big round of applause. Chino's eyes were glued to Ericka, stepping offstage. She made her way through the crowd, saying thank yous to the compliments she received. Chino watched her go to the bar.

He stood. He had to know. No matter what, he needed to know if they shared a connection. He strode towards the bar, sliding in beside her. Ericka ordered a glass of Patron. Chino spoke up, "Put that on my tab." Both Ericka and the bartender, a thirty-something black guy, turned to look at him. Chino was trying to look cool, not looking at her.

"You got a tab?" asked the bartender.

Chino handed him his platinum card. "Make it so, number one." The bartender looked at the card and shrugged. "I'll have a whiskey, rocks," said Chino. The bartender nodded and went off to prepare the drinks.

Chino turned towards Ericka now, raising his left eyebrow in that way women always liked. He grinned. He held his hand out. "Nice to meet you. I'm Chino."

She smiled awkwardly. He could tell she was unsure, but she shook his hand. "Chino, huh? Where'd you get a fancy five dollar name like that?"

"My pops was a Charles Bronson fan."

"I don't know who that is."

"Who? Charles Bronson or my pops?"

She smirked a smirk that said he was corny.

"Charles Bronson was an actor," he said. "*Chino* was a movie he was in that came out the year I was born."

"I'm named after somebody famous, too."

"Yeah?"

"Ericka Huggins. I'll bet you don't know who that is."

"This might surprise you, but I do. Ericka

Huggins was a Black Panther. Got arrested along with Bobby Seale."

She lit up. "I'm shocked."

"You didn't think a white guy would know about that?"

"These days, half the black folks don't know that."

He started to speak, but the bartender came back. Chino and Ericka both smiled and took their glasses.

"So what, Charlie Bronson?" she asked. "What do you want?"

"I just wanted to meet you."

"What's so great about me?"

He didn't know what to say, so he blurted out, "*Everything.*" Ericka looked startled, and he felt embarrassed. "Not that I know you," he said, backpedaling. "You just seem..." He wanted to say perfect, but instead said "really cool."

She smiled. "You know what, Charlie? I *am* cool."

"You wanna sit down and finish this conversation?"

She gave him a strange look, but relented, her features loosening. "You payin' for the drinks?"

He nodded, grinning. "All the drinks you want."

She looked at him suspiciously. "You tryin' to get me drunk, Charlie? Are you gonna take advantage of me?"

"I just wanna get to know you."

She shrugged, looking radiant as she did. He saw that gleam in her eyes again. That gorgeous, heart-melting gleam that lit up already beautiful eyes. "I got nothin' else goin' on. Where you wanna sit?"

Chino turned and looked. He saw an empty table right smack dab in the middle of the crowded room. He hated crowds and usually avoided such placement, but right now he didn't care. All he could see was her. "How about that one?"

She nodded and they moved to the table, sitting next to one another.

"What do you do?" she asked.

"I'm a mechanic."

"That pay well?"

He shrugged. "I eat."

She took another drink. Chino asked, "What do you do?"

She gave him a look like he was stupid. She nodded towards the stage. "What do you think *this* is?"

"This is cool, and you're good at it, but this don't pay bills. Maybe one day, but not today."

"Why you think that?"

"I used to do standup," he said. "I worked the clubs."

She lit up. "No shit?"

"No shit."

She looked at him, sizing him up. "You don't look like a comic."

"What does a comic look like?"

She thought about it. "I don't know. The only comics I've ever seen were black comics. I don't really go to comedy clubs."

"Maybe you should."

She deflected him, saying, "Maybe."

"Tell me something," he said.

She looked him in his eyes. "What?"

"You said I don't look like a comic. What *do* I look like?"

She smirked. "You look like a cop."

He frowned. "That's fucked up. Why I gotta be a cop?"

She laughed hysterically. "You're not a cop?"

"Trust me, girl, I am *not* a cop. Call me anything. I mean it. Call me a motherfucker, an asshole, a peckerwood white boy. Anything. But not that. Not a fuckin' cop."

"You don't like cops?"

"I fuckin' hate 'em."

"My cousin Sharice is a cop."

He didn't know what to say. Then, thankfully, she said, "I never did like that bitch. When we was kids, she was always tellin' on everybody. No wonder she became a cop."

Chino chuckled.

She asked, "I know why I don't like cops. I don't like 'em because I'm black. But why don't you like 'em?"

"For the same reasons you don't. The way they treat black people is awful. Everything from that 'stop and frisk' bullshit to that cop shooting Orlando Castille in front of his daughter. And the cop got off."

"They always get off." She looked at him, studying him. "What's with your ear?" she asked. "Why's it look like that?"

Chino hated this question and had spent most of his life trying to forget he was missing half an ear.

"Oh, that," he said. "I got in a fight with a motherfucker when I was a nineteen. We got into it and got to wrestlin' around on the ground. I was really givin' it to him, punchin' him over and over in the ribs."

"Then what?"

"Motherfucker bit off part of my ear."

"Like Mike Tyson," she said.

Chino nodded. "Fuck Mike."

"So what happened to the guy?

"The cops showed up and everybody scattered. He got away, and I never saw the motherfucker again."

"I'll bet you think about him a lot."

"Every goddamn day."

"What was the fight about, anyway?"

"Funny thing is, that fight changed my life, but I don't even remember what it was about. We were playin' basketball. Probably somethin' somebody said."

"Was it you?"

"Probably." Chino grinned. "But I didn't deserve this."

"I think it's kinda cute, Charlie Bronson."

"I was thinkin'."

"Yeah?"

"I was wonderin' if I could be somethin' else? You know, instead of a cop."

She grinned. "What do you wanna be?"

"Literally anything else."

"Okay," she said, grinning. "I know what you can be."

"What?"

"A country singer. You can play the banjo and all that shit."

He stared at her, watching her giggle.

"Now you're just fuckin' with me," he said.

"You're intentionally naming every fucked up white guy occupation there is."

"I'm sorry, Chino," she said, calling him by his actual name this time. "I was just playin'."

He grinned. "I'm not offended."

"That's good."

"Why's that?"

She smiled a great big smile, holding up her glass. "So you can order me another drink."

Chino grinned. He finished his and stood up. He went to the bar, got fresh drinks, and returned. He handed her the Patron.

"You seem like a nice guy," she said.

"There's a reason for that."

"Yeah?"

"It's because I am."

"Every guy says that. I'll bet Harvey Weinstein says that." She paused. "I don't know if you know this, but men lie."

"That's news to me."

"How 'bout you? Do you lie?"

"Sure, I lie. Just not about this."

"Then what *do* you lie about?"

"I lie about lots of things."

"Tell me about your lies."

"I went to the movies the other day and the kid at the register asked me if I was a veteran."

"So you lied?"

"I became an ex-Marine and saved myself two bucks."

"But you're not lyin' about this?"

"I'm not."

"Look, Chino, I like you. I really do. But I don't really..." She paused, and Chino prepared himself for a letdown. "I don't date white guys. I mean, I think you're cute and all."

"And funny," he said.

"And funny. But I don't... I never dated a white guy before."

"You don't like white people?"

"Not always, no. I got nothin' against 'em, but most of them got somethin' against me. When you've lived your whole life with white people callin' you names and followin' you around the store, afraid you're gonna steal somethin', you develop a distrust. But it's not all white people. I mean, I got a girlfriend who's white."

"Ah," Chino said. "The old 'I've got a friend who's your color so I'm not racist' bit."

She frowned. "I read people pretty well. I like you. I've known you for a total of twenty minutes, but I dig you."

"But you won't date me?"

She looked him in his eyes, deathly serious. "If I dated a white guy, my parents would kill me, Chino. They were very militant, very pro-black. They raised me that way. I try to see the best in people, and I like you a lot, but my parents would have a heart attack." She paused. "Correction. They would kill me first, and *then* they'd have a heart attack."

"Maybe they'll like me."

"You don't know my daddy. I assure you he would not."

Chino sighed. He tried to lighten the mood. "Who said I was gonna ask you out anyway?"

She smiled and stood.

"It's been nice meeting you, Chino."

"You performing tomorrow?"

"You gonna come?"

"I might be in the neighborhood."

"I'll be here."

They both smiled.

He said, "Maybe our paths will cross again."

"Is that a threat or a promise?"

"Which would you prefer?"

"You need to know somethin' right up front."

"What's that?"

"Even if you come back tomorrow, we can't date. We can be friends, but we're not gonna date."

Chino smiled and winked. "We'll see."

SIX

He'd spent the day dreaming about her. He couldn't help it. Somehow he'd already fallen for her. This left him with two challenges. The first was to convince Ericka that he was the man of her dreams, and the second was to somehow talk Cocoa out of having her killed. He wasn't sure which one would be the hardest.

Meeting Ericka felt like kismet. Chino didn't know if he believed in God and had never really cared one way or the other. But if there was a God, Chino hoped he would give him this. Just this one thing. Chino had been a bad man and had done bad things, but he believed he'd paid his penance. And if he saved Ericka, that had to count for something.

Tonight would be a make-or-break situation. It could change the course of his life. Was he prepared for this? He didn't know, but he was willing to take the risk. He felt bad for Aliesha, but she wasn't coming back. He checked himself in the mirror, thinking he looked good. He was wearing an old school Adidas jacket—the one with the stripes on the arms—and a Wu-tang tee underneath.

He arrived at Henry's a little bit later than he had the night before. The place was even more packed tonight. He approached the same bartender, who grinned. "You lookin' for Ericka, huh?"

Chino just said, "Whiskey. Rocks."

"You gonna run a tab?"

Chino nodded. As the bartender went to fix his drink, Chino fished out his credit card. As he waited, he looked around. He didn't see Ericka, but he did see a Puerto Rican cat they called Straw Man that he knew from work. Straw Man was a heavy. After he got his drink, Chino approached his table. Straw Man looked up at him.

"Hey, Chino," he said. "How's tricks?"

Chino shrugged. "Same shit, different day."

Straw Man motioned towards an empty chair. "You wanna sit?"

Chino did. "You here for work or pleasure?"

"Work. Waiting for the motherfucker owns the place. He owes Jimmy Balls a chunk of cash."

"Big chunk?"

"Big enough."

"So you gotta rough him up?"

Straw Man nodded. "Boss said break out his teeth."

"All of 'em?"

"That's what the man said." He sat there considering it. "Shit. I didn't ask for specifics. I just assumed. And you know how that shit goes..."

"I do."

"Jimmy didn't say whether I should bust 'em all out or just a few."

"I'd break 'em all."

"You think?"

"Better safe than sorry. Jimmy ain't gonna care if the guy ends up with too few teeth. But he's gonna be upset if you leave too many."

Straw Man nodded. "You're right. Jimmy don't fuck around."

"That's what they say."

"You know why they call him Jimmy Balls?"

"No," said Chino. "I never heard."

Straw Man leaned in, like he was telling a secret, but when he spoke it was still loud. "Back in the day, he made a name for himself by cuttin' off guys' balls."

"That would do it."

"People tend to remember that shit."

"You think it's true?"

"It seems like something he'd do. Jimmy got a temper like nothing I ever seen before. When I was in the joint, I was there with this big Nigerian dude named Bingo."

"B-I-N-G-O?"

"Bingo was his name-oh. Motherfucker was vicious. He was a fuckin' cyclone, makin' his way through the yard, leavin' dudes on the ground."

"Dead?"

"Nah, he just beat the hell out of 'em," said Straw Man. "But word was he'd killed some guys in Harlem over a drug deal went sideways. You know how them Nigerians are."

"Nah," said Chino. "Never met one. None that I know of anyway."

"Nigerians don't fuck around. And this cat Bingo was the worst. He was a tough sonofabitch if there ever was one. He'd just as soon break your neck than look at you."

"Yeah?"

Straw Man nodded. "And as scary as Bingo was, Jimmy Balls is ten times worse. Maybe more. I know he looks old, but he's ruthless."

"That's the word I heard." Chino sat there, sipping his drink. "Can I ask you a question?"

"What?"

"Speakin' of how guys got their names, how'd you get yours?"

"It's a bullshit name. I wish there was a cool story. Sometimes I think about it and think maybe I should make one up. About how I killed a guy with a straw or some shit. Some John Wick shit, you know? But it ain't nothin' interesting like that. What it was was, when I first started workin' for Jimmy, back in the day, I used to smoke."

"Yeah?"

"Three packs a day."

"Cigarettes ain't cheap."

"Fuck no," said Straw Man. "So when I finally quit, I started chewin' straws, tryin' to replace the cigarettes. Motherfuckers would see that shit and call me Straw Man. After a while, it stuck. So here I am twenty years later, don't smoke, don't even chew straws, but everybody calls me Straw Man."

"There's worse names, I guess."

"One time Jimmy sent me after a guy. You know what his name was?"

"No idea."

"Guy's name was Little Dick Brown."

Chino stared at him. "That sounds like bullshit."

"It can sound like whatever, but I'm tellin' you, his name was Little Dick Brown."

Chino shook his head. "Let a motherfucker try and call me some shit like that."

Straw Man chuckled, taking a drink. As he did, the emcee from the previous night made his way onstage. "What's up, y'all?" he asked the crowd.

The audience livened up, clapping and cheering.

"You motherfuckers havin' a good night?"

The crowd cheered.

"Y'all ready for my girl, Ericka?" The crowd cheered and the emcee winked. "You know she's my future wife, right?" There was some laughter. "She don't know yet, but it's gonna happen one of these days."

Now Ericka stepped on stage, shaking her head. She took the mic and looked at the crowd. "Not in this lifetime." Everyone laughed. Ericka said, "How's everybody feelin' tonight?" The crowd cheered and Ericka introduced a black guy sitting behind the drums and the Latina at the piano.

"This next song is an old one," Ericka said. "Maybe you know it." The piano player started to play, and a moment later the drummer joined in. "This song is 'You Don't Own Me.'"

She was halfway into the song, Chino hanging on her every word, when Straw Man said loudly, "That bitch is fine!" Chino just nodded and let it go.

Ericka sang ten songs, closing with "I Would Die for You." When she closed, she thanked everyone for coming out. She blew the crowd kisses, and everyone clapped and cheered. As she stepped offstage, Straw Man leaned in again. "Man, she's somethin' else. What I wouldn't do for a piece of that." No sooner than he'd said this, he turned to see Ericka standing behind them.

Chino said, "I didn't think you saw me."

Straw Man was confused, looking back and forth between them.

"Of course I saw you," she said. "You mind if I sit?"

"No, no," said Straw Man. "Go ahead, sit your fine ass down, girl."

Ericka sat, giving Straw Man the stink eye.

"What's that look?" he asked.

"It means fuck off," she said.

Straw Man looked wounded, saying, "I know when I'm not wanted."

"I'm glad you cracked the case, Einstein. It wasn't supposed to be a secret."

Straw Man stood, looking at Chino. Chino just shrugged. Chino extended his fist. "You and me, we still good?"

Straw Man gave Ericka a pissy look. Then he turned back to Chino, giving him dap. "Yeah, we good." He mean-mugged Ericka one last time and walked away.

Ericka looked at Chino. "Who was that clown?"

"Just some guy."

"A friend of yours?"

"Nah, more like a friend of a friend."

"You should get better friends," she said. "You gonna buy me a drink?"

Chino grinned. "All night long."

Ericka winked. "You know what I drink."

"Don't go anywhere." He stood and she said, "I wouldn't dream of it."

Chino went to the bar and got the drinks. It took a few minutes, Chino having to wait behind a group of drunk women ordering slowly and asking questions. Finally he got the drinks and brought them back to the table, sitting down.

"You said you were a comic," said Ericka.

"I did."

"Then tell me a joke, funny man."

"Nah."

"Come on. Prove that you're a comic."

"I *was* a comic."

"Just tell the joke."

He shook his head. "When people come up to you, spur of the moment, and ask you to sing a song, what do you do? Do you do it?"

She smiled and started singing "If I Ever Fall in Love." The impromptu performance was perfect—as good as anything she'd done on stage. But this one was special. This one was just for him.

"Fine," he said. "I'll tell you a joke."

"I'm all ears."

"Why does Santa Claus have such a big sack?"

"Oh, my God... Why?"

"Because he only comes once a year."

Ericka giggled. "Okay, Charlie Bronson. That was funny."

He shrugged. "It's what I do."

"Tell me another one."

He looked at her with disbelief. "You asked me for a joke, I told you a joke. I'm not doin' a whole routine."

"Please," she begged.

"One more joke. But that's it."

"One and done," she said.

"One more joke..." He thought about it for a

moment. "Okay, what's the best part of sex with twenty-eight-year-olds?"

She stared at him, waiting for the punchline.

"There's twenty of them!"

She shook her head. "Damn. That's bad."

"Those are the kinda jokes I told."

"I don't think I woulda liked your comedy."

He shrugged. "Those kinda jokes aren't for everybody."

"That was pretty offensive."

"Obviously you know I'm not fuckin' eight-year-olds, right?"

She nodded.

"It's just a joke. It's meant to be audacious. Yes, it's fucked up. But look, P.C. ain't funny. It just ain't."

"Do you tell race jokes?"

"No," he said. "Cross my heart, hope to die. That's not my thing. I'm not a bad guy. I just tell jokes. It's like Stephen King."

"How's that?"

"He writes violent shit, right? But he doesn't actually do it. He's not condoning violence. He's just tellin' a story. Well, that's how it is when you're a comic. You're just trying to entertain."

"I guess. But that's not really my thing."

"I'm sorry."

"Nah," she said. "It's not a big deal."

"So we're still friends?"

She grinned. "You keep buying drinks, we'll be whatever."

"You mean that?"

She got serious. "I'm like you—I was just jokin'. You're not fuckin' eight-year-olds and I'm not..." Her words trailed off.

"Fuckin' me?"

She nodded.

"Who said I wanted to fuck you anyway?"

SEVEN

Chino woke up in Ericka's bed, their naked bodies intertwined. It took him a moment to remember where he was. He turned his head to face her. Her eyes were closed and her breath was warm. Her eyes opened with perfectly-choreographed timing. She smiled, saying, "Hey, you."

"How you feel?" she asked.

"I feel like I got run over by a truck."

"I'll bet."

Chino's skin felt cool beneath the fan overhead. Her smell—something sweet and wonderful—was in his nostrils.

"Weird question," he said. "What kind of perfume you wear?"

"Why?"

"You smell good."

Her smile became a smirk. "You gonna run out and get you some, so you can smell good too?"

"Maybe."

"You're a lucky man, Charlie Bronson."

"I know," he said. "But why do you say that?"

"I don't usually bring gentlemen callers back to my place."

He grinned. "That what I am? A gentleman caller?"

"You're no gentleman. A caller, maybe, but not a gentleman."

Chino looked up at the fan. "You got me."

"Seriously, this never happens."

He turned to face her. "No?"

"No. I'm a good girl."

"No, you're not. I know better."

"I've got appetites and urges like anybody else."

"You're a wild animal," he said.

"Maybe."

He looked at her, serious now. "You can be my wild animal."

She rolled her eyes. "Remember—just friends."

"I got news for you. Friends don't do what we just did."

"No?" she asked. "What about that guy in the club?"

He thought about it for a moment. "*Straw?* No, we *definitely* don't do this." He looked at her. "How about you? Do you have sex with your friends?"

"I have."

"Male or female?"

"What do you care?"

"How about white guys. You been with any others?"

"Just one."

"Before me?"

"The guy's name was Dennis. We went to college together. We were on the school paper."

"You were a journalism major?"

"I was," she said.

"What you do now? You a journalist?"

"I work in a pharmacy."

He grinned. "You're a drug dealer."

"How about you? What's your story? Are you married?"

He looked at her and she saw the pain in his eyes. He didn't want her to, but she did.

"What is it?" she asked.

"I was married once. I had a family. A wife

and two kids. They were beautiful. They..." The words hung there, and he started to cry.

Ericka sat up on her elbow, staring at him. "What is it?"

"They're...*gone*," he managed. He hated himself for crying but couldn't stop it. "They're dead. They were on the highway, and a vehicle swerved into their lane. I..." He couldn't finish. Even after all these years, their deaths remained an open wound.

Ericka leaned in and kissed his forehead. "Baby, baby," she whispered. "It's okay."

But it wasn't, and it never would be. Not for Aliesha. Not for his babies. All the thoughts and prayers in the world couldn't bring them back. They were gone—nothing left but ashes.

Ericka pulled him close and held him as he wept. At this moment, they weren't new friends or lovers; it felt like they'd known each other forever. "I'm sorry," she whispered.

He pulled back and looked into her eyes. "*I'm* sorry."

She looked at him with motherly, consoling eyes—the same look Aliesha had given him when his father died. "There's nothing to be sorry about."

They lay there, holding each other for a good half hour. Finally, Ericka sat up. "You hungry?"

"I could eat."

"I make a mean omelet."

"Oh, you're fancy."

"You think an omelet is fancy?"

"Most days I just eat Fruit Loops."

"Fruit Loops?"

"Not always. Sometimes I get fancy too."

She grinned. "What do you eat?"

"Cap'n Crunch."

She laughed.

"Fancier than that," he said. "Not just regular Cap'n Crunch."

"Crunch Berries?"

"You know it."

"You're a basic motherfucker, Chino."

He laughed, looking at her sitting on the side of the bed. "You're gorgeous, you know that?"

They stared at one another for a long moment. "You really like me, huh?"

"I do," he said. "And I don't like anyone."

"Get out with that shit."

"I'm serious. My wife Aliesha died eight years ago..."

"Eight years?"

"Eight years, two months, and three days. Guess how many women I've dated in those eight years?"

She stared at him.

"Just you," he said. "You're the only one."

"Is that what we're doing? Are we dating?"

"I'd like to date you."

Ericka stared at him, her expression a mixture of concern, confusion, and stress.

"What are you thinking?" he asked.

"This was a mistake."

This hurt, striking him like an arrow, straight to the heart.

"Really?"

She turned away, sliding her legs around so they hung off the side of the bed. She looked down, trying to figure things out. He sat up, reaching out to touch her shoulder. She didn't resist, letting him rest it there. He could see her trembling, and he knew she was crying.

"Ericka?"

She said nothing, so he sat in silence, unsure what to say. Finally, he repeated himself. "Ericka?"

She turned to face him. There were tears in her eyes. Staring at her, he thought she looked beautiful. Most people ugly-cried, but not her. She was even more beautiful now than she'd been before. It was her vulnerability. This tough woman, always in control, had let her guard down, allowing him to see the real woman beneath.

"I love you," he said. He knew he shouldn't have said it. It was way too early to say it, but it felt right.

"No, Chino," she said quietly. "I can't."

"Why?"

She pulled away, letting his hand drop. She stood. "I told you why. I told you." There were still tears in her eyes, but she wiped them away defiantly. Her walls were back up again. "I don't date white guys."

"I think you like me."

"That's not the point."

"Then what is?"

"You don't even know me. How do you know you love me?"

"I've only felt this way about one other woman, Ericka, and that was my wife."

She huffed and rolled her eyes. "Come on. I'm sure that took a while, right? This is... This is too quick."

"I proposed the first week."

"How long were you married?"

"Nine years. We're only apart now 'cause she's dead."

"You just *knew*? Like what, in your gut?"

"In my heart," he said. "And guess what?"

She was standing there with her arms crossed, ready to fend off the words she knew were coming. "That's how I feel about you." She was trying to look tough, but he could see her eyes starting to glisten.

"You gotta go," she said.

"Ericka, come on."

Her expression didn't waver. "Seriously. You gotta go."

He sighed. "Okay." He would not beg. He wanted to, but begging now would be a waste of time and could potentially make things worse. Maybe there would be a chance another day. But time was running out.

She watched him get dressed. He made his way through her apartment. He went to the front door and opened it. She was right behind him. He stepped out onto the stoop. He turned to look at her. "I'm sorry, Ericka."

She closed the door.

EIGHT

Chino and Dobbs were shooting pool. Grillby's was nearly empty, B.B. King playing on the jukebox.

"This is what you get," said Dobbs.

Chino, stick in hand, about to shoot, looked up. "For what?"

"For fallin' in love with your mark, dumbass."

Chino did a half-shrug and leaned in, taking the shot. He tried to hit the three in the corner but missed.

"Riddle me this, Batman," said Dobbs. "How does a motherfucker fall in love with somebody he barely knows?" He was frowning, visibly irritated.

"I know her. We slept together."

"Dammit, Chino. I've slept with hundreds of bitches."

"Hundreds?"

"Ain't you?"

"Not even close."

Dobbs raised his finger to make a point. "We're gonna get back to this, rest assured. But my point was that I've had sex with hundreds of women, and I ain't never fell in love but once, maybe—and I mean *maybe*, because I still ain't sure—with two women total. Ever. And that shit didn't happen in two days. Not even close. And even then, after years—*literal years*—I didn't *wanna* fall in love."

"You couldn't help it."

"I see what you're doin'."

"But that's what happened. I'm tellin' you. I didn't go lookin' for this. It happened to me! You know that thing where Malcolm says 'We didn't land on Plymouth Rock, Plymouth Rock landed on us'? Well, that's what it was."

"She landed on top of your dick?"

"I wouldn't put it like that."

"But you in love."

"You don't have to agree with it, but I'm askin' for advice."

"You don't want my advice."

"Cause you gonna say what?"

Dobbs stood there for a minute, staring down at the pool table, pretending to be looking for his shot. He looked up. "You got two options." He paused. "Well, three counting what you supposed to do."

"The other two?"

"Those are easy. You either convince Ericka to run away with you and go somewhere far away. Go off someplace and live a nice, quiet life —bullet-free. And then there's the other option."

"Which is?"

"You could kidnap her."

"*Kidnap her?* That's extreme."

Dobbs gave him a sideways look. "The whole fuckin' thing is extreme. This is a big no-no. This ain't how it's done. You're the best hitter in the city. Maybe the east coast. The go-to guy when somebody needs popped. But you do this, your life won't be worth a popsicle in a snowstorm. You gonna be through. Most likely dead." He looked at him, pleading now. "It ain't too late, Cheen. You can turn this around. You can turn this whole ship around and just go the other way. You clip her now, nobody would ever know."

"I can't do that, Dobbs."

"Then hell, let *me* do it. Let me put a bullet in her. I'll do it right now, at this moment. I'll walk out this bar and go fix the whole thing right now. I won't tell nobody it wasn't you. Nobody'll know. Just us, and we'll never speak of it. Not a fuckin' word, Cheen. Not one."

Chino stood there, looking down at the table. "No, Dobbs. She lives."

Dobbs was getting pissed now. "Here's a scenario for you. Let's say you go and spill your guts out to this bitch and make one last plea for her affections. Say you go and say the sweetest shit a motherfucker ever said to a bitch. What happens if she don't wanna be with you? Then what? You gonna throw away your life for someone who doesn't wanna be with you?"

Chino nodded. "I think so."

Dobbs threw up his hands. "You a dumb motherfucker. I thought you were smarter than this. I thought I taught you better. I don't have friends, Cheen. Not really. But you and me, we're bonafide road dogs. But..."

"But what?"

"As your friend, it's my job to tell you the truth."

"And the truth is?"

"I told you the truth."

"That it's dumb to fall in love?"

There was fire in Dobbs' eyes. "That it's dumb to let this bitch live. I know it sounds harsh, Cheen, but this is your job. This is what you signed on for. This is who you are. You kill people."

"I do, but that's not who I am."

"You really believe that? When you're a hitter, you're defined by your job. You gotta be. Once you've killed ten or twelve people, there ain't no comin' back. It's who you are. It takes hold of your soul, and it blackens it. You're a killer, Cheen. It's who you are, whether you like it or not."

Chino looked him in the eyes. "I can't hurt her."

"So you just gonna piss it all away, just like that?"

"There's another option."

"How you see that?"

"Maybe I go talk to Cocoa and convince her to call this off."

"Oh, that what you gonna do, Cheen? You gonna just sit down with her, maybe have some tea and crumpets... exchange pleasantries. Then, while you're at it, just sorta slip it into conversation? 'Hey, Cocoa, I got a question. You know that bitch you want me to kill? Well, here's the thing: my dumb ass fell in love with her. I wanna run off and marry her. She don't love me though. But it don't matter. So hey, could you do me a solid and not kill that bitch? If you could do that for me, that would be great." He stared at Chino. *"Do you hear how stupid that sounds?"*

Listening to Dobbs say it like that, it did sound stupid.

"But it might work, Dobbs. You don't know."

"Dammit, man. Don't do this. You're gonna get killed. I don't wanna see that happen." His voice wavered, deathly serious. "I only got one friend, and unfortunately that friend is your dumb ass. Please don't get killed over a piece of ass. Please don't do this."

"She's more than a piece of ass."

"I can see you love her. Fine, you got my blessings. Whatever. I'll even stand up in your wedding. I don't care. But you be careful. Don't get fucked up."

Chino grinned. "You worried about me?"

"No, I'm worried about me, dummy. 'Cause if you do this... if you run off and play Captain Save-a-Hoe... if Cocoa and her goons come after you..."

"What?"

"I'm gonna have to get involved. And I don't wanna get involved. I'm retired. I ain't supposed to be playin' shoot-em-up with Cocoa and her stupid goons. I'm supposed to be..."

"What?"

"Doin' retirement shit."

Chino grinned. "Like what?"

"I don't know, but it sure as hell ain't shootin' up a bunch of dumb motherfuckers 'cause you a sucker for love."

"I'm sorry, man."

"Your ass better be."

They both chuckled.

Dobbs looked at him. "You know how you can make this up to me?"

"How's that?"

"You can buy me a drink."

NINE

Chino was outside Ericka's place, sitting in his Beamer, waiting for her to come home. It was pouring rain and Chino was wet from when he'd knocked on her door, finding her gone. Sitting there, he knew the optics were bad. She would come home and think he was stalking her. And he was, he supposed, but not in that way. He was trying to save her, even if she didn't want saved.

The afternoon was gray. The rain pounded as if God was taking a piss after holding it a while. Finally, after Chino had waited several hours, a black Ford Escape pulled up and stopped. Chino watched Ericka climb out, waving goodbye to the older black man driving. Chino guessed it was her daddy.

Ericka's umbrella opened the second she stepped out, and after waving, she made a mad dash to her door. Chino watched the man drive away. Here goes nothing, he thought. Chino got out. He didn't have an umbrella and he thought covering his head would be futile. He didn't run. He strode through the rain, as if he didn't have a care in the world. But he did. He had a lot of cares and a lot of worries.

By the time he reached the stoop, Ericka had already disappeared inside. He walked up the steps. He took a breath, clenched his fist, and pounded on the door, semi-hard but not cop-hard.

He saw the peephole darken. There was a long moment before the door cracked open. Ericka stared at him through the chain-lock.

"*What the hell, Chino?*"

"We need to talk."

"I told you to stay away."

"Technically you didn't. You just said leave. You didn't say it was forever."

Her eyes were fiery. "I thought you understood. What do I gotta do? Write it out for you? I don't wanna see you anymore. I had my doubts, and your coming here now in the fuckin' rain... First you say you're in love after one night—*one fuckin' night*—and then now, here you are, standin' on my doorstep in the pourin' rain. Your shit is tired, Chino. You gotta go."

"I think my love scares you."

"You're goddamn right it scares me."

"So what?"

She looked him in the eyes. "You gotta go."

Before he could say anything, she started to shut the door. He had to act. It was now or never. He pushed his shoulder forward and banged hard into the door, snapping the chain. Ericka fell back against the wall. Chino barged in, towering over her. She was still standing, but cowering, and he knew she was afraid.

"It's not what it looks like," he said.

"It's not?" she screamed. *"'Cause what it looks like is you're a goddamn psycho!"*

Chino remained calm. He closed the door. He turned around and looked at her. "There's somethin' you need to know."

She stood her ground, but Chino grabbed her arm. She tried to push him away, but he kept his grip. He nudged her towards the front room. She relented and they walked together. When they reached the front room, he released her arm. "I need you to sit and listen," he said. "After that, if you want to tell me to go get fucked, you can. But until then, I'm askin' you to sit down, shut up, and listen."

She looked at him, still defiant and angry. "You some kinda tough guy, Chino? You get your kicks pushin' women around?"

He sighed. "You know me better than that."

"No, I don't. I don't know anything about you."

He motioned towards a recliner and told her to sit. She did. "What is this?" she asked. "You gonna rape me?"

"If I was gonna rape you, I would have done it."

"Oh yeah?"

He held up his hand, gesturing her to be quiet.

"Just shut up for a minute. I realize this goes against everything you know, but please, for just this minute, shut up and listen."

She stared at him.

"Remember when I told you I was a mechanic?"

She nodded. "I do."

"Well, I lied."

"Why?"

"Do you know what a hitman is, Ericka?"

"*What the hell?* This is a joke, right?"

"It's not a joke. I'm really a hitman."

"So...you...you *kill people?* For a living?"

"I know how it sounds," he said.

"It sounds fucked up."

"It's not as bad as it sounds."

"How's that? Do you or do you not kill people for money?"

"I do, but it's not how you think."

"Then how is it?"

"I do kill people, and I do get paid. But it's not really that bad."

"How?" she asked. *"How is it not that bad?"*

"The people I kill are bad people." He looked at her and remembered why he was here. "Well, *most* of them are bad people."

"How are they bad?"

"I work for an organization."

"Like the mob?"

"Sorta," he said. "But it ain't like you think. It ain't like John Gotti and Al Capone—all the Italian stuff."

"What do you mean?"

"It's different now. It's... diversified."

She didn't understand.

"Take my boss for instance. She's black."

She clapped her hands sarcastically. "Bully for progress. I guess this is what Martin died for, huh? So a black woman could be a crime boss."

"None of that matters right now."

"Then tell me what does."

"You."

She rolled her eyes. "Give it a break. Tell me why we're here."

"If you'll give me a chance, I'll tell you."

"Okay, shoot."

"This time the assignment was different from the others. I didn't want it."

She tried to understand. "What do you mean?"

"I always had one rule. I would never kill a woman. This time, the mark was a woman. An *innocent* woman. Normally, they're criminals and bad guys. When they get clipped, fuck 'em, no big loss. They deserve it. It costs big money to have somebody clipped, so rest assured they did somethin' wrong."

"Okay?"

"The target is you."

She looked like she'd been slapped. *"What?! Are you serious?"*

"I'm here to protect you."

She studied him. "You don't know me. Why would you do that?"

"Because I love you."

She threw her hands up, becoming angry and animated. "'I love you,' says the guy sent to murder me." She looked at him again. "Why me? What the fuck did I do? Why would anyone spend money to hurt me?"

"Because of your dad."

"*My dad?* What did he do?"

"I don't know, but there was somethin'. The boss said she wanted to teach him a lesson." He stared at her. "What does your dad do?"

"He's an alderman. Thirty-sixth district."

"He's the reason we're here."

She gave him an angry look. "But you're gonna save me, huh?"

"If you let me."

"You know what this sounds like?" she asked. "It sounds like you're creating a problem so you can swoop in and fix it. This crime boss thing is probably made up." She stared at him. "You probably don't even have a gun."

He pulled back the jacket, revealing the .45 in its shoulder holster.

"How many people has that thing killed?"

"None yet. They give me a clean gun everytime they send me out."

"Oh goodie," she said. "Then I get to be the first one you shoot with it."

He leaned down and grabbed her shoulders, shaking her. This startled her, but there was no time to fuck around. "I told you I'm not gonna hurt you," he said. "But you've gotta listen to me. Whether you like it or not, you're in danger. I'm not gonna kill you. But if I don't do it, she's gonna send somebody else."

"Then what good is your not doing it?"

"You don't understand. It's not that I'm not gonna kill you. I'm gonna *save* you."

"From all of them?"

He nodded. "I'll shoot every motherfucker who comes after you."

"*Why?*"

"Stop asking. You already know."

"This doesn't make sense."

"Lots of things don't make sense. Add this to the list."

She stared at him in silence for a beat. Finally, she said, "Won't this get you in trouble?"

He stared into her eyes. "Yes, it will. If I do this, we'll both have targets on our backs. They'll shoot me the same as they'll shoot you."

"So what's the point? If they're gonna kill us, what good is this?"

"Because I'm better than them," he said. "I'm better than everyone she's got. She might hire out and get somebody else, but I'm the best in the city."

He thought she looked slightly impressed but figured he was misreading her.

"I'll throw it all away for you," he said.

She stared at him, and it appeared it was

starting to sink in. Feeling tired, Chino sat down across from her. But as he did, Ericka suddenly bolted out of her chair, hurtling towards the door. Chino leaped from his chair, giving chase. When she fumbled with the door, he dove towards her, tackling her hard. He tried to hold her down, but she bit him on his forearm, drawing blood.

"Jesus!" he screamed. "Why you gotta make this so hard?"

TEN

CHINO CARRIED Ericka through the downpour, feeling glad for the rain. If it wasn't for that, someone might notice Ericka with a sock stuffed in her mouth with her hands and feet tied. She bucked in his arms, her eyes big and angry, but he kept moving towards the car. Opening the trunk with her in his arms was difficult, but he managed. Once the trunk was open, he set her inside. She fought her restraints, mumbling inaudible obscenities as loudly as she could.

"Sorry, Ericka," he said as he closed the trunk.

He started the car and maneuvered through the streets, his wipers barely keeping up. He could hear her banging around, so he turned the stereo up. He was playing De La Soul. Chino was stressed and tired, and he nodded his head to the rhythm as he drove.

What would he do now? He didn't know. And now she would definitely hate him. She probably thought he was a kidnapper. But then, he was, wasn't he?

Twenty minutes later, he pulled up in front of Dobbs's little pink house. He hit the button to call his friend. Dobbs answered on the third ring.

"What the fuck, man?"

"It's Chino."

"I know who you are. My phone's got caller ID, same as everybody else's. What you need?"

"You alone?"

"Why you ask?"

"You got a woman in there?"

"Yeah. There's a woman here."

"She an important woman?"

Dobbs chuckled. "Not anymore."

"What's that mean?"

"We done already fucked."

"Damn, man," said Chino.

"So what? What you need?"

"I'm outside."

"Okay?"

"I need to come in, but I can't do it with her there."

There was a pause. "No askin' or nothin'? Just 'I'm comin' in'? You got nerve, Cheen. It important?"

"Extremely."

"Why can't she be here? What do you care? I'm the one who should be mad about her, not you. If you saw this bitch's face... She's a closing-time pickup if there ever was one."

"That ugly?"

"You don't even know."

"It's business."

"Gangster shit?"

"Definitely gangster shit."

"Damn, Cheen. Gimme a minute." Chino could hear Dobbs yelling. All he could make out was "you gots ta go, bitch." He heard the woman yelling but couldn't understand the words. Then Dobbs said, "Save that shit, and get the fuck out!" The woman cursed some more and then Chino saw the front door open. A half-dressed middle-aged black woman with a bad wig emerged. She was still yelling, and now Dobbs was standing on the porch wearing boxers and an open robe. Dobbs was shooing her away. The woman stalked through the rain towards a red Toyota parked in front of Chino. When she reached the car, she turned and yelled again. Dobbs just stood there laughing and waving.

The woman banged her fist on the top of her car, got in, and sped off.

Chino switched off the ignition and "Baby Baby Baby Baby Ooh Baby" shut off abruptly. Now Chino could hear Ericka banging around in the trunk again. He stepped out into the rain. When he stood, he looked at Dobbs, standing on the porch,

"What the fuck, man?" yelled Dobbs. "It's too early for this shit."

Chino headed towards the trunk and popped it open. When he did, Ericka lunged at him. Somehow she'd gotten loose. Before he knew what was happening, she was on him, scratching his face with her nails. The pain was immediate, and it stung like hell. He grabbed her, shaking her, the two of them face to face.

"Jesus Christ, Cheen!" Dobbs said.

Chino ignored him, still staring at Ericka. "This is for your own safety. Unless you want a bullet in your head, you'll cooperate." She became quiet and still. "The bullet won't be mine. Whether or not you wanna believe it, there are some people who are real pissed at your daddy. They want you dead. Unless you do as I say, you're gonna be dead faster than Nicholas Cage can make ten movies."

She stared at him. He was still holding her, but she'd stopped fighting.

"What if I don't go peacefully?" she asked.

"Then I'll knock your ass out. I won't like it, and you won't like it. I won't wanna do it, but I swear to God I'll do it."

She stared at him, looking tired. "Where we goin'?"

He looked at Dobbs on the porch.

Ericka looked too. "Who the hell's that?"

"He's gonna help us."

Ericka nodded and started moving towards the porch. Chino looked at Dobbs. "You done went too far," said Dobbs. "Why you bringin' this bitch to my house? She got a target on her head. If you want one on yours, that's you. But I don't."

As they approached him, Dobbs kept ranting. "Jesus Christ, Chino! I swear you're dumber than a box of rocks."

Chino gave him a look and said, "We'll talk about it in the house."

"You got-damn right we gon' talk about it."

Ericka said, "So everybody's crazy here."

Dobbs gave her a hard look. "Ain't nobody crazy but lover-boy here."

Dobbs was holding the door for them. Chino turned towards Dobbs, and Dobbs ripped into him. "Motherfucker, I taught you better than this. You just like my got-damn kids, Chino; ain't none of 'em listen. They ask for my advice, I give it to 'em, then they do the exact opposite. I told you to put a bullet in her head." Dobbs caught himself and looked at Ericka, putting his hand up to calm her. "Ain't nothin' against you, girl. Nothin' at all. It's the job." He looked at Chino. "And you know the job, Chino. You know how it's done, and this ain't it! Cocoa asks you to clip somebody—" Dobbs looked at Ericka. "Even if it's a fine-ass bitch like this, you do it. That's your job. That's literally the whole fuckin' job."

"So what?" asked Chino.

"So you fuckin' up, Cheen. You fuckin' it all up. You know what's gonna happen now?"

Chino stared at him.

"You gonna get popped for this." He looked at Ericka. "And she gonna get popped." He looked at Chino again. "I oughta fuck you up, you know that? Because it ain't gonna just be the two of you that gets popped. I'll get popped for helpin' your dumb ass."

"I won't let that happen."

"How you gonna do that, Cheen? You gonna rewrite the gangster handbook? You gonna change all the rules 'cause you in love?"

Ericka said, "The feeling is *not* mutual."

Dobbs stared at Chino. "There you have it,

straight from the girl's mouth. You gotta kill her. You got no choice. You can't throw away your life over some bitch who don't even like you." He looked at Ericka. "Again, it ain't you. Chino's just a dumbass."

She shrugged. "I'm aware."

Now Dobbs turned his wrath towards her. "No, I don't think you do. This motherfucker here, dumb as he might be, is literally killin' himself to save your ass. Do you know anything about Cocoa?"

"I never heard of her," she said.

"Let me tell you about her. She's the boss of New York City. And you know how she got there? She didn't get there through affirmative action. It wasn't just hard work. It was because she kills motherfuckers. She kills her competition. Anyone who gets in her way. She don't pull the trigger, but she calls the shots. So if she sets her sights on somebody, they dead. That's how it is. And guess what?"

She said nothing.

"She wants your pretty ass dead. Dunno why, don't care. It ain't our job to care. People like us, we just do what we're told. The boss says bust a cap in somebody, we do it. Like it's nothin'. We do it like it's any other nine-to-five job, like we bankers and lawyers. We put in our time and we clock out and go home." He paused. "At least that's how it's supposed to be." He looked at Chino with disdain. "But that ain't good enough for Chino. Nah, he had to go and fall in love. And if you don't get it, that fucks things up."

"Why do you care?" she asked.

"I care 'cause this dummy's my friend." Dobbs walked over to a coffee table with a pistol on it. He reached for the gun. "If Chino won't do it, I'll do it myself." He picked up the gun and turned towards Ericka, finding that Chino had his own gun trained on him.

"Don't," said Chino.

Dobbs stared at him, a tired expression on his face.

"I'll kill you, Dobbs," said Chino. "I love you, but I'll shoot you deader than Tupac."

His gun still trained on Ericka, Dobbs looked at Chino. "Why you doin' this?"

"'Cause I love her." His voice sounded weak and sad, but it was clear he would shoot Dobbs if pushed to.

"You know what this is?" asked Dobbs. "This some bullshit." He sighed, lowering the gun. He looked at Ericka. "You better be worth it."

ELEVEN

They were sitting in Dobbs' living room, talking it out. No one was fighting or trying to get away. Chino had expressed a need for whiskey, and Dobbs had supplied it. They all had drinks now. Chino was drinking whiskey. Dobbs and Ericka had screwdrivers.

Ericka was sitting forward, holding her drink in both hands. "If this is real, where does this put us?"

"In a world of shit," said Chino.

"Right," said Dobbs. "It puts us in a world of shit."

"What does this have to do with my daddy?" asked Ericka.

"It means he's dirty," said Dobbs.

"Maybe he's not dirty," said Ericka. "Maybe that woman's just tryin' to get him to do somethin'."

"Nah," said Dobbs.

"If Cocoa wants you dead, there's more to it," said Chino. "Cocoa wouldn't just jump right to killin' the guy's daughter. His hands are already dirty."

"Daddy wouldn't do that."

"You don't know shit about your daddy," said Dobbs.

She looked at him. "Neither do you."

"Nobody knows nobody. I heard a story on the radio about a motherfucker—family man, you know. Guy spends Thanksgiving with his family. Eats turkey, makes some jokes, maybe watches some football. But then he leaves, says it's for work. He goes out to a buncha porno shops and sucks a buncha glory hole dicks. One after the other."

"What the fuck kinda radio you listen to?" asked Ericka.

Dobbs grinned. "The point is, nobody knows nobody. Not really. We grow up thinkin' our parents are one way, but really, they're a whole other thing. We think there's no way they could cheat on each other, but really, Daddy's bangin' half the bitches he works with. I got kids, Ericka. You probably didn't know that."

"How could I?"

"Thing is, I was a contract killer for a lotta years. But my kids never had a clue. You think they believe their pops put fifty-three people in the ground?"

Ericka's jaw dropped. *"You killed fifty-three people?"*

Dobbs chuckled, taking a drink. "Ask lover boy here how many people he's killed."

Chino shrugged.

"My point remains," said Dobbs. "Nobody knows nobody. I read a story about an old disabled guy who died penniless. His family had no idea, but now they think he might'a been D.B. Cooper." He looked at Ericka. "You know D.B. Cooper?"

She scowled. "What kinda dummy you think I am? He hijacked a plane and stole a shitload of money. Then he jumped out with a parachute and disappeared."

"Well got-damn, Cheen!" said Dobbs. "You got a smart one here."

"He ain't got shit," said Ericka. "We ain't together."

Chino looked into her eyes. "Let's get this clear, Ericka. Whether you like me or not don't matter. You better learn to play nice, because I'm the only thing between you and a bullet."

Dobbs nodded. "He's right. It was me, you'd 'a done been dead."

Ericka asked, "How many people you kill, Chino?"

"Sixty four," he said. "You were supposed to be sixty five."

She blinked. "You killed sixty-four people, but you wanna save *me*? What makes me different?"

"You know."

"Because you love me," she said. "But how do you *know*? How can you possibly know that?"

"Don't matter," said Dobbs. "Just be happy he does, for whatever reason. I may not believe in love at first sight—you may not believe in it, either—but you best be glad he does. 'Cause if it was me—or literally any other hitman sent to get you—you'd be dead. So he's right. You don't have to like his dumb ass, but at least respect him savin' you."

"It doesn't make any sense," she said.

"It don't make sense to me either," said Dobbs. "But you know what? I'm not half the man this motherfucker is. 'Cause he's got more compassion and empathy than I got. What I say won't change anything, but you'd be lucky to have him in your life."

She considered this. She looked at Chino sheepishly. "I'm sorry," she said. "I don't understand any of this. But if what you've said is true, then thank you."

"We ain't in the clear yet," said Dobbs.

"Miles to go," said Chino.

"So what do we do?" she asked.

Dobbs sat back, jiggling the ice in his empty glass. "We're gonna have to get you out the city."

"*Leave?*" she asked.

"What?" asked Dobbs. "You wanna stay and die? That don't sound like a good plan to me."

"What about my parents?"

"Don't contact them," said Chino. "Not yet."

"Your daddy is the reason you're here," said Dobbs.

"I'm gonna talk to Cocoa," said Chino.

Dobbs looked at him. "You gonna kill her?"

"Nah. She been good to me."

"You think she gon' be good to you after this?"

"Prob'ly not. But maybe I can talk her outta killin' Ericka."

Dobbs looked skeptical. "I've only met that bitch a couple times, but between what I've seen and what I've heard, she don't strike me as a real understanding person. This ain't gonna go well. You motherfuckers ain't gonna end up holdin' hands and singing Kumbaya."

"Maybe," said Chino.

"Maybe my ass. She gonna end up killin' both your asses. She gon' kill us all. All this because you *in love*."

Chino nodded. There was nothing to say. Dobbs could guilt-trip him all he wanted, but it wouldn't change the way he felt.

"I'm gonna call her," said Chino.

"I guess it's worth a try," said Dobbs. Chino thought he was being sincere, but then Dobbs added, "Maybe you could take that bitch a cheese tray. Maybe send her some roses."

Chino had his phone out now.

"I love you, man, but you're a fool," said Dobbs.

Chino dialed the number. The phone rang twice before Domino answered.

"Yeah?" said Domino.

"This is Chino. Let me speak to Cocoa."

"She's lookin' for you. She's unhappy."

"Well, she ain't gotta look no more, 'cause I'm here. So if she's unhappy, you can put her on the phone and she can tell me herself."

"Always a cool guy, huh, Chino?"

"I was you, I'd go get the lady."

"Or what?"

"You know what. And you won't like it. Now get Cocoa."

There was a moment of silence. A moment later, Cocoa was on the line. "I been lookin' for you, Chino. Where you at?"

"I haven't been hidin'."

"But you haven't done what I told you to do."

"That's the thing..."

"There's a thing?"

"I've worked for you a long time. Done a lotta jobs."

"A lotta good work," she said.

"Sixty-four jobs."

"Supposed to be sixty-five."

"I wanna talk about that."

"Why, Chino? We never talk about it. Why we we talkin' now?"

"I wanna ask you for a favor."

"You do, huh?"

"I wouldn't say we're friends, you and me."

"You don't think we're friends?" she asked.

"But I think we respect each other."

"That's true, I guess."

"How many favors have I ever asked you for, all the time I've known you?"

"None."

"Right," he said, "None."

"But you're askin' now."

"I am."

"It's your rule about killin' women, right? You want me to send somebody else."

"No," he said.

"Then what?"

"I want you to stop this. I don't want you to kill her."

The phone went silent. Finally, Chino said, "You there?"

"Why you askin' this?"

"I've got my reasons."

"You pussy-smitten? That it?"

"Please," said Chino. "If you respect me, you'll consider this."

"Don't put me in this position," she said. "I respect you, but this ain't a road you wanna go down."

"You told me this wasn't anything she did that got her into this," Chino said. "It was to teach her father a lesson."

"The reason don't matter."

"Just listen."

"No," said Cocoa. "You listen, and you listen close. I'm givin' you one chance to fix this. It's not too late. You kill the bitch, you and me are solid."

Chino stared at Ericka. Was she worth all this?

"You hear me, Chino?" asked Cocoa.

Staring at Ericka, Chino knew she was.

"I won't kill her," he said.

"Didn't your mama teach you to look both ways before crossin' me?"

"If you respect me," said Chino, "I'm askin' you—"

He heard a click. He looked at Dobbs.

"She hung up?" asked Dobbs.

Chino nodded.

"What does this mean?" asked Ericka.

"It means shit's about to get real," said Chino.

"This is one of them 'from bad to worse' scenarios," said Dobbs.

"I figure we sit tight and figure out a plan of attack," said Chino. "We gotta figure out where we can take her so she'll be safe."

"Even if you hide her, she won't be safe," said Dobbs.

"I know," said Chino. "You get her outta the city. I'm gonna go see Cocoa."

TWELVE

Chino was sitting Indian-style on the floor, admiring Ericka. Ericka was stretched out on a ratty old couch. Dobbs was sitting in a tattered recliner. Dobbs watched Chino take a swig from the whiskey bottle.

"If you're gonna do this, you need to lay off that shit," said Dobbs. "You need to be sharp."

"This is how I do it," said Chino. "I never kill anybody sober anymore."

"I hate to interrupt all this," said Ericka. "But I got a job. I got responsibilities. I can't just leave. What am I supposed to do?" She thought about it for a moment. "I don't even know what you're saying is true. This could be bullshit."

"It ain't bullshit," said Dobbs. "There's a

mean bitch out there who wants you dead. But..."

"What?"

He grabbed his pistol and raised it, showing her. "Chino wants you alive, so I'm gonna make that happen. You ain't gotta like it. I could give a fuck less. But you goin'."

"*Couldn't* give a fuck less," she said. "Everyone says it wrong."

"You know what?"

She stared at him.

"I *couldn't* give a fuck less what you think."

"Okay, so where we goin'?"

"That's the million dollar question," said Chino. "Where can we take her?"

"I'll figure it out," said Dobbs. "I don't know where she gonna be safe."

"I'll take care of it," said Chino.

Dobbs stared at him. "I know your ass, Cheen. You gonna go in and threaten her. Tell her to back off. But you need to really *do* the thing, Cheen. This ain't no go-halfway shit. This is a go-all-the-fuckin'-way-and-then-some situation. This is do-or-die. You gotta put a pullet in her head. You let Cocoa live, you gonna pay." He looked at Ericka. "You'll both pay."

Chino nodded, thinking about it.

"I know where I can take her," said Dobbs.

"My uncle Deke got a farm upstate. I'll take her there and we'll lay low 'til we hear from you."

"Thanks," said Chino.

"I got your back," said Dobbs. "I'ma always have your back."

"And I got yours."

Ericka looked at the two men. "Are you two gonna suck each other's dicks now?"

They both turned and looked at her, shaking their heads.

"Okay, first thing's first," said Dobbs. "I gotta make a call."

"Your uncle?" asked Ericka.

Dobbs shook his head. He picked up the phone and pressed a button, raising it to his ear.

"Hey, Bolo?" he said. "Yeah, this ya boy Dobbs. I gotta place an order." There was a pause. "Yeah, the usual. But this time I need three."

Chino and Ericka looked at one another.

"*Three,*" Dobbs repeated.

Chino and Ericka watched attentively.

"Sure thing," said Dobbs. "You know where I live."

Dobbs switched off the phone and looked at them.

"Guns?" asked Chino.

"Nah, nigga. Chinese takeout."

Chino stared at him, confused. *"You think we got time for that?"*

"Don't go off half-cocked, Cheen," said Dobbs. "Sit your ass down and eat before you go do this. Besides, me and Ericka got a five hour drive. We're gonna need to eat. It ain't like we can just stroll into Taco Bell and place an order."

"So you ordered Chinese?" asked Ericka.

"I ordered Chinese," said Dobbs.

"How you know it's safe?" asked Chino.

"I order that shit every day."

"Every day?" asked Ericka.

"Sometimes twice a day."

"That shit ain't healthy," said Chino.

"Anybody ever tell you about MSG?" asked Ericka.

"Fuck MSG," said Dobbs. "If the six motherfuckers done shot me ain't managed to kill my ass, MSG ain't gonna do it either."

"You been shot six times?" asked Ericka.

Dobbs grinned. "I got a talent for it."

"But we're safe?" asked Chino.

"Hell yeah. My nigga Bolo, Chinese guy, runs the place. He delivers my shit every day. I know the guy. He ain't mobbed up. Hell, he can barely speak English." Dobbs sat there, grinning. "He don't know much English, but goddamned if he don't know them curse words. Got them down real good. Likes to say 'motherfucker'. Sounds funny when he says it. You should hear him."

"I'll bet he learned half those words from you," said Chino.

Dobbs shrugged. "I do tend to rub off on people."

"Can we go by my place so I can grab some clothes?" asked Ericka.

"No," said Chino.

"We go to your place, we gonna get more than clothes," said Dobbs. "We go there, we gonna get shot all to hell."

"What about feminine products?"

Dobbs looked at her. "You on your period?"

"No," she said. "But I coulda been."

"But you ain't, bitch."

"You gonna pack a bag?"

"Ain't shit to pack."

"You just gonna wear the same clothes?"

"If lover boy does his job, we won't need clothes. We won't be gone long. Besides, all I need is toothpaste and a toothbrush."

"How about your gun?" she asked.

Dobbs grinned. "Never leave home without it."

The three of them discussed the situation and exchanged snarky remarks for twenty minutes until they heard a knock at the door. Everyone tensed. Chino and Dobbs reached for their guns and stood. "I got this," said Dobbs, his pistol raised and ready. He went to the door and peered through the peephole, relaxing.

"It's just Bolo." He pulled the door open, and they saw a heavyset Chinese man holding two white plastic bags.

"My nigga!" said Dobbs.

Bolo smiled and started to say something—maybe motherfucker—but was stopped by a bullet in the back of his head. The shooter used a silencer, so it took a moment to register as they watched Bolo's eye explode from its socket. A millisecond later, Dobbs saw the white gunman emerge, and he suddenly felt pain in his shoulder.

Dobbs cried out, wheeling around.

Chino's gun was up, aimed at the gunman. It was a motherfucker named Hans who worked for Cocoa. Chino squeezed the trigger, and the bullet struck Hans in the cheek, dropping him. Chino looked at Ericka. "You stay here."

Ericka looked at Dobbs. "You okay?"

"Can't you see, bitch? I been shot."

Ericka looked at Chino disappearing through the door.

"Where's he goin'?" she asked.

"After the other guy."

"There's another guy?"

Dobbs nodded. "When they send Chino, they don't use a second guy. They don't need him. Chino's like me—a one-man band. But with these other hitters..."

"They send two guys."

"Exactly."

"Chino must be pretty tough."

They heard a man scream outside. Then, suddenly, the guy stopped in mid-scream. Dobbs grinned. "That Chino, he's a fuckin' Terminator. Toughest white boy I know. I said it before, but you could do worse."

She rolled her eyes. "I got it the first time."

Chino came through the door. "Remember that guy Junebug I told you about?" he asked.

"Fat brother, got braids?" asked Dobbs.

"Yeah."

"Was that him screamin'?"

"It was, but his screamin' days are over."

Dobbs smiled. He stepped outside, stepping over Bolo's body, and picked up the sacks. "I guess the food's free tonight."

"What about tomorrow?"

"Let's try to live through today and then we'll see what happens tomorrow," said Dobbs. "The motherfucker who shot me looked foreign. Maybe European."

"You caught that in that half-second?"

"It's what I do. That's why I was good at this."

"I'm gonna go see Cocoa and fix this," Chino said. "You two get on the road, head up to Uncle Zeke's."

"Uncle Deke," Dobbs corrected.

"He could be Uncle fuckin' Sam for all I care. Just get her outta here. Keep her safe."

The two men stared at one another.

"You good?" asked Chino.

"Right as rain," said Dobbs. He looked at his wound. "Except for this bullet in my shoulder."

"That makes seven," said Ericka.

"Like I said, I got a talent for it."

Chino grinned and headed for the door.

"Keep your ass safe," said Dobbs.

Chino, at the door, stopped and turned around. Ericka thought he was gonna come back and kiss her. She was prepared to be angry, but he didn't do it. Instead, he went back for his bottle. Watching him go, Ericka realized she was disappointed he hadn't kissed her.

THIRTEEN

CHINO MADE his way through the city, heading towards Cocoa's place. It was night, and Tupac was on the stereo rapping "Hail Mary." But Chino wasn't listening. He was lost in thought, considering the possibility he might die soon. And if he died, Ericka died. And Dobbs too.

Was Ericka worth it? Was *anyone* worth dying for? A person who didn't even like or care about him. The answer was obvious, but Chino chose to ignore it. But really, what was the point? It was unlikely they would ever be lovers. *Maybe* friends, but not lovers. But did it matter? Or, more to the point, *should* it matter? If there was nothing in it for Chino, why do it? He could stop it now if he chose to. But he wouldn't. Ericka was a good person who didn't deserve to die. And he loved her.

Now he considered all the previous marks he'd killed. Had *they* deserved to die? Yes, he told himself. Yes, they did. Most of them were gangsters, so it was on them. If you don't wanna die like a gangster, don't be a gangster. But had there been others like Ericka who were simply collateral damage? It was likely. But none of it could be changed now.

But *this* could. Couldn't it? Thinking about it, Chino wasn't sure. If he put a bullet in Cocoa's head, he'd have to put a bullet in the heads of everyone she worked with. Because *someone* would come after him. That's how it worked in this business.

He was close to Cocoa's place now. There was very little traffic.

Chino's heart was pounding so hard he thought it might burst out of his chest. He'd killed a lot of people, and he'd never felt like this. Even in the beginning. He'd been nervous, sure. He'd even puked after his first hit. But it hadn't been like this. This was different. This was overwhelming fear and anxiety. He wasn't so much afraid of dying as he was having to kill Cocoa and her soldiers. Once he started down this path, there would be no turning back. He would be a marked man. If he killed Cocoa, he and Ericka would be looking over their shoulders for the rest of their lives.

Was there another way out of this? Could he convince Cocoa to just let them go? It seemed unlikely. Even if he convinced her give Ericka a pass, his own life would be forever changed. He couldn't go back to work as though nothing had happened. This was a game-changer. This was one of those three or four moments where, if you lived long enough, you would look back on for the rest of your life. This would be a pivotal moment that would change everything that followed.

Chino parked down the street from the apartment building to keep from being spotted. The street was empty and no one was milling about. Looking two blocks down to Cocoa's building, however, he could see two goons standing watch.

Fuck 'em, he thought.

Walking towards them, striding as if he hadn't a care in the world, Chino knew they didn't have walkie-talkies. He hoped they wouldn't recognize him until he was too close for them to do anything. Then he'd have them. But if they recognized him before that, he would be made. One of the fuckers would run upstairs and tell Cocoa, and then all hell would break loose.

Walking towards them, still a full block away, he could see they hadn't spotted him yet. They were standing there shooting the shit, absorbed in conversation. He could see one of them clearly. It was Marky D. Marky was one of those guys, Italian, about Chino's age, who looked like he'd been a bad motherfucker once upon a time. But age and weight had done a number on him. Now he had that Harvey Keitel old man body—a fair amount of muscle and lots of flab. The other goon was a younger fella. Real skinny motherfucker. One of those bland, nondescript white guys nobody noticed.

Chino crossed the street. He was less than a block from them now. It was quiet—as quiet as things ever got here. There were white noise sounds of traffic and horns in the distance, but that was it. The two goons were still talking, paying no attention.

He moved towards them, closer and closer, his pistol at his side. Fifteen feet now. Ten. Five. One of the goons—the one facing him—noticed Chino. His eyes got big and he started to move. There wasn't time for him to tell Marky. Chino raised the pistol before the guy could get his. Marky started turning just as Chino squeezed the trigger. He shot the guy in the nose. Marky saw this, heard the zip, and knew. *"Please,"* he managed. Chino fired again, catching Marky in the eye.

Chino approached the dead bodies, towering over them. He raised his pistol and put another round in each for good measure. He turned and opened the door.

FOURTEEN

Dobbs and Ericka were halfway to the farm, and the drive had already taken its toll. Dobbs didn't like long trips and said so repeatedly. He was driving his old Ford Explorer, and Ericka had offered to drive, but he'd refused.

They'd spoken very little and what had passed for entertainment had been Dobbs singing along to Teddy Pendergrass. He'd told her about the three times he'd seen Teddy perform live. "Back when he was alive," he'd said, as if Ericka might have mistakenly thought he'd seen a ghost concert.

"It Don't Hurt Now" was playing when Ericka asked Dobbs, "How long you and Chino been friends?"

"A few decades, I suppose."

"You said you used to be a hitman, too. Why'd you quit?"

Dobbs chuckled. He looked at her with a gleam in his eye. "I was real good at that shit," he said. "I'm serious. I was like Teddy here. I was the Teddy fuckin' Pendergrass of hitmen." Hearing his own words, he chuckled again. "I was *good* at it. But it wasn't the kinda job I felt good about doin'. My mama, God rest her soul, she woulda up and died all over again if she'd known what I was doin'. Everybody got that one thing they're real good at. Sometimes it's a thing you really wanna be good at, and then other times it ain't. But I was so good, I didn't wanna stop. I was like Hammer—too legit to quit."

"But you did."

"I sho nuff did," he said. "Killin' a motherfucker's hard. *Real* hard. Thing is, it ain't so much the work that's hard. That shit is easy peezy. Like I said, I had a talent for the game. But livin' with it is the hard part. It's like those soldiers who come home from the war and they got PTSD from all the people they killed." He turned towards Ericka. "Bein' a hitter is like that. It's like war. Some big-shot fancy-pants motherfucker sends you out to shoot somebody, and you do it, no questions asked. You do it 'cause you're a soldier. You convince yourself what you're doin's right. You're just doin' your job. It ain't personal. That's what you tell yourself. But that ain't the truth. Takin' a motherfucker's life is about the most personal thing there is. So I would go to sleep, and I'd have nightmares. I'd see the marks' faces. Same dream, every night."

As he said this, his expression became pained.

"It's their faces right before you shoot 'em," he said. "It's them frightened, lookin' at you, beggin'." She heard his voice crack. "They wanna pay you to save 'em. All of 'em." He looked at her. "Bein' a contract killer pays well, but a nigga could make a big score takin' one of those payoffs. You could make a million easy." He looked at her. "Thing is, motherfucker might come back and fuck your shit up. You see that movie *Miller's Crossing*?"

She told him she hadn't.

"Good movie," he said. "It's got John Turturro, the dude plays the racist Eye-talian in *Do the Right Thing*." He turned towards her again. "You *have* seen *Do the Right Thing*, right?"

She told him she had not.

He looked at her with a crazy expression. "Damn, Ericka. What the fuck are you doin' with your life?" He looked back towards the road, taking a moment to collect himself. "*Miller's Crossing* is a movie about a hitter who lets his mark go. He ain't even make no money off it. You believe that? But the motherfucker he lets live comes back, fucks it all up." He was silent for a moment. "Truth is, the motherfucker ain't even gotta come back. You could let a guy live and he goes off to Belize, somebody sees him, you still end up dead. It ain't worth it. Money ain't everything. I'd rather be alive and broke than dead and rich."

"But there were nightmares."

"*So many nightmares*," he said. "I couldn't deal with 'em anymore."

"How about Chino? He have those nightmares?"

"Every motherfucker does what we do has 'em. It's as much a part of the job as guns and marks."

"That why he drinks?"

Dobbs grinned, but not like he thought it was funny. It was a tired, sad grin. "Chino drinks because his wife and kids died. He tell you about 'em?"

"A little, but not much."

"He loved them more than *anything*. He was

talkin' 'bout leavin' the life way back then, but never got around to it. His wife, Aliesha, was his *everything*. He loved her more than I ever saw a motherfucker love a woman." He looked over at her to see if she understood. "She never did know what Chino did."

"How is that possible?"

"I'm sure she knew he was doin' some foul shit on the wrong side of the law. But people tell themselves whatever they have to to convince themselves things are how they want 'em ta be. It's like when a husband cheats, and the wife tries to convince herself it ain't happenin'. That's how it was. She knew, but she didn't *wanna* know."

"What did she think he did?"

"He told her he worked in construction."

"And she believed it?"

"She did." He smiled, staring at the road ahead. "Thing is, Chino was never dirty. Always came home clean. One day, she asks him why he's always clean, he tells her it's because he's the foreman."

"What was Aliesha like?"

He grinned. "She was a lot like you. She didn't look like you or anything like that. She was athletic. Mixed girl. Mama was white, daddy was Jamaican. Whip smart." He looked at her. "That's how Chino likes 'em, you know? Smart."

"And you don't?"

"I don't care all that much. I just like 'em breathin' and not complainin'. Problem is, them things are mutually exclusive. Ain't many women breathin' who ain't complainin'."

"That's sexist as fuck."

"Nah. That's just truth."

"What else?"

"She was a writer. Wrote children's books."

"What were they about?"

"One of 'em was about a giraffe," he said. "And you know what? She named the motherfucker Dobbsy." He nodded his head happily, looking at the road. "So now, as long as I live, somewhere out there some kid is readin' a book about Dobbsy the motherfuckin' giraffe."

"What were her other books about?"

"One of 'em was about their kids. The characters had the same names, and the art looked just like 'em. They was goin' on adventures. Went to the moon, I think. Aliesha only wrote one of those before the accident, but it was supposed to be a series."

"What were their kids like?"

Dobbs lit up, smiling. "Tyrese and Kailee. They were the best-behaved, sweetest kids. They were like family. Even called me Uncle Dobbsy." His voice cracked again. Ericka thought he might cry, but he didn't. "If you'da known Chino back then... He had a light... a *spark*. Somethin' I haven't seen in years." He looked at her. "Until you showed up." He continued. "Man, Chino loved them kids. Did all kindsa shit with 'em. All the normal daddy shit. I wish you coulda known him then." He was smiling, looking ahead. "But I guess that wouldn'ta worked, would it?"

She wanted to tell him she didn't care about Chino. But it wasn't true. She'd only known Chino for a short period of time, and yet he'd put his neck on the line for her. No man had ever sacrificed anything for her. Especially not like this. But it wasn't every day a crime boss tried to kill her.

"Why do you think he's hung up on me?"

Dobbs grinned, turning towards her. "You ever look in the mirror?"

She smiled. "There are plenty of women who look prettier than me. And Chino doesn't even know me."

"If it was me, I wouldn't look a gift horse in the mouth. Chino wants to save you, so just let him do it and say thank you."

"That doesn't mean I owe him."

He looked at her like she was nuts. "You

don't gotta be his girlfriend, but you *do* owe him. You literally owe him your life."

She wanted to argue and tell him all the reasons he was wrong, but she couldn't think of any. Instead she said, "I didn't ask for this."

"I didn't ask for this either. But here we are."

FIFTEEN

Chino stepped inside the building and saw Chuckles O'Malley sitting in a chair to his left. The old Irishman wasn't much in the way of security, sitting there reading a *Spiderman* comic. Chuckles glanced up nonchalantly, doing a double take. Chino had his pistol aimed at him.

"What's up, Chino?"

Chino responded by putting two slugs in Chuckles' chest. Before Chuckles' body hit the floor, Chino was already at the elevator, pushing the button. It took a couple minutes for the elevator to arrive. Chino kept his eyes on the front door, watching for more goons. It occurred to him that Cocoa might have a surveillance camera here, so he looked around but saw none.

The elevator opened. Luckily, it was empty. Chino stepped in and pressed the button. There was some Michael Buble shit playing; a terrible cover of an old song Chino had hated even before Buble fucked it up worse. When Chino reached the penthouse, the elevator door slid open, and there was Dameon's big ass. He was just standing there, arms crossed, looking tough for no one. Their eyes connected, and Chino's pistol was already up.

Dameon played it cool. Both of them knew what time it was. Dameon nodded. "'Sup, Cheen?"

"You already know."

"You sure you wanna do this? I mean, we could just fight it out, man-to-man. No guns."

Chino smiled. "Why the hell would I do that?"

Dameon nodded. "Can I ask you a favor?"

"What?"

"Not my face, okay?"

"Your face ain't that pretty."

Dameon smiled. "I know, but I want an open casket. For my kids."

Chino obliged, putting two rounds in his chest. Dameon toppled back, sliding down the wall. Seeing this, Chino felt a wave of sadness. He'd always liked Dameon. He was a good dude, and none of this was his fault. It was Cocoa's. Chino ejected the clip from his pistol, replacing it.

Knowing Domino would look through the peephole, Chino lifted Dameon's body, heavy as fuck. Chino's pistol was still in his hand. He slid Dameon over in front of the peephole so Domino would think it was him. Knocking on the door with this heavy sonofabitch in his arms was hard, but Chino managed. He saw the peephole darken, and a series of locks started to click. Chino dropped Dameon. The door swung open and there was Domino, looking at him with a shocked expression like he'd just seen Big Foot butt-fuck his mother.

"Chino," he managed. "It's... *you.*"

Chino's gun was in his face. "Who were you expectin', the Easter Bunny?"

Domino looked terrified. He made a strange face and looked down. Chino looked too, seeing Domino had pissed himself.

"Damn, Dom," said Chino. "This ain't your day."

Domino looked up, simultaneously frightened and embarrassed. "You gonna kill me?"

"Let me in, you fat fuck."

Domino stepped inside, and Chino strode in, his gun still in his face. "You try anything, they'll be cleaning pieces of your brains off the walls for weeks. Not that you got any. But whatever you got in that skull of yours, it'll be on the wall." Dom didn't move, didn't say shit. Chino looked around. The front room was empty.

He told Dom to close the door. Dom did this in silence.

Chino motioned towards the plush chair he'd sat in when he'd been here last. "Sit your fat pissy-pants ass down and keep your mouth shut." Domino did as he was told.

"Domino, get me a drink, darling," Cocoa said from the next room. Chino watched the door where he'd heard the voice, and Cocoa emerged. She stepped out, distracted, putting on a big gaudy earring as she did. She looked up, saw Chino, and dropped the earring.

"Jesus Christ," she said.

Chino smiled. "Not quite."

Cocoa looked at Domino. "Why the fuck you let him in?"

"He, uh... tricked me."

"Shut your dumb ass up!" she snapped. She turned towards Chino, her eyes narrow and fiery. "So what, Cheen? What you gonna do, huh? You gonna shoot me?"

"I should."

"That don't answer my question."

"You and me are gonna have a talk."

He motioned towards the couch with the pistol. "Sit." She did.

"The way I see it, we got two options," Chino said.

"That's how you see it?"

She stretched her arm across the top of the couch cushions, trying to get comfy, like she was settling in to watch a movie. She didn't look like she was in danger. Cocoa was that cool.

"Well," said Chino. "I could kill you."

"You could." Their eyes were still locked. "Tell me, Chino. How would you do it? Where would you shoot me?"

"In your face."

This seemed to startle her, and Chino wondered what response she'd expected. But she snapped back into the moment, as cool as a cadaver. She smiled. "Okay, what else?" she asked. "What's the other option?"

"You could let Ericka live."

Cocoa laughed a hard, genuine laugh.

"That funny to you?" asked Chino.

"What happened to you, Chino?" she asked. "You were the best there was. You were unstoppable. I needed a job done, I could count on you getting' it done. And now, *what?* You're *in love* with this bitch? This ...*singer*." She said it like it was a bad word.

"I asked you not to send me."

"But I did. I sent you. I sent you to do a job you were apparently incapable of doing. You turned soft."

"Everybody falls in love."

"You think?"

"What?" he asked. "You never been in love?"

"I dunno. Once, maybe."

"Yeah?"

"I was married once. Long time ago. It's true. His name was Donnie Gammon. He was a small-time hustler in Harlem. Numbers, girls, dope."

"And you married him?"

"I did," she said. "It was a warm Saturday in June. Outdoor wedding. Really pretty, like in the movies."

"What happened?"

"He cheated on me."

"And?"

"I did what I do to everybody who lets me down."

"You killed him?"

"He went missin' one night. No one knew where he'd gone. The cops thought maybe he'd run off with one of his whores. But he didn't.

Not really. They found him about a year later, but his head was gone." She stared into Chino's eyes. "They never did find his head."

"That supposed to scare me?"

"I don't give a fuck what it does."

"Let Ericka go."

"Or what?"

"You die. Right here. Right now."

"Yeah?" She looked unimpressed.

"Maybe I make you suffer first. Maybe I put the first one in your shoulder. Shoot a few bullets here and there, make you hurt. Then work my way up, keepin' you alive. Maybe I shoot you in the throat."

She shrugged. "I've lived a good life."

"And you still can. Just let the girl go."

"And what about you, Chino? What am I supposed ta do with you?"

"You let me go too."

She laughed. "And what will you do? Go to work at Wal-Mart? Chino, this killin' thing is all you got. It's all you're good at. I mean, what else you gonna do? Tell your jokes?"

"I'm askin' you to let us go so I don't have to kill your ass."

He could see she was considering this, turning it over in her head.

"You come after us, I'll come back here," he said.

"And kill me."

"Not just you. Everyone. Everything you love."

"I don't love anybody."

He feigned pain. "You don't love me no more?"

"You got balls the size of King Kong comin' here and talking to me like this. I respect that."

"Enough to let me live?"

"If I let you live, it's got nothin' to do with respect."

"What then?"

"Maybe I got shit left to do. Maybe I ain't ready yet."

"So you'll let us go?"

"If I do this," she said, "you gotta leave the state. Both of you. And you can never come back."

"To the *whole state*?"

"You're lucky it ain't the planet."

"Not ever?"

"Come back and see what happens."

"But if we leave and never come back?"

She sighed. "If you walk away and leave New York..." She stared at him. "And put away your guns and leave this life behind, I'll leave you be."

"You promise?"

She grinned, crossing her chest. "Cross my heart and hope to die, Chino. That make you feel safer?"

It didn't. He considered shooting her anyway but knew he couldn't. If he killed Cocoa, he'd never stop running. Chino was tired. He didn't feel like running.

"I'm tellin' you, I see one of your goons anywhere near me or Ericka, I come back here and you all die."

She chuckled. "All *who*? The whole city?"

"Pretty much." He backed towards the door.

"I better never see you again."

"You better hope so too," he said. He felt the doorknob against his back. He reached back and grabbed it. He pulled the door open and backed out. He waved to her with his pistol. "Bye, Cocoa."

"Fuck you, Chino."

He closed the door. Cocoa looked at Domino, looking nervous in his piss pants.

"What the fuck, Dom?"

"I'm sorry, boss."

"You *are* sorry," she said. "Sorry as fuck."

He lowered his head like a sullen child.

She sniffed the air. "What's that smell?" She looked around for a moment. Then she looked at him. "Did you piss yourself?"

He nodded, a sad look on his face.

"You still packin'?" she asked.

"Of course."

She held out her hand. "Let me see the gun."

"Why?"

"Let me see it."

Domino stood and held out the pistol, placing it in her palm. She looked at him with fire in her eyes.

"Goddamn you, Domino!"

She aimed the pistol and fired center mass, shooting Domino over and over again until the pistol clicked empty. She sat there, staring angrily at the dead bastard. Seeing his dumb, blood-covered face made her even angrier, and she hurled the pistol at him.

ACT TWO

SIXTEEN

Every AA meeting was the same. Chino would sit and listen to everyone's stories, many worse than his, and he'd keep his mouth shut. But today was different. Today he would speak for the first time.

Everyone sitting at the two tables was staring at him, waiting to hear what he had to say.

Today, he was grinning. He held up his five-year coin, showing it off like a child who'd just won a prize at the arcade.

"My name is Chino, and I'm an alcoholic. Today is my five-year anniversary being sober." Someone down the table, across from him, started clapping, which led, gradually, one additional clap after another, to everyone clapping.

"Happy birthday," said Ted, an old real-estate agent who'd been his sponsor.

Chino beamed. "I haven't felt like I've earned a lot of the things in my life, but I've earned this." He paused, looking down, feeling his eyes starting to glisten. He looked up. "My wife Ericka is one of those things I never earned. Without her, I wouldn't be here." He paused, trying to collect himself. "And I don't just mean here, receiving this coin. I mean *alive*."

Looking around, Chino saw a few of the other alcoholics nodding with understanding. "When I met her, I was a different person," said Chino. "I wasn't all that great. Hell, I'm pretty far from great now, but I'm better with her by my side than I was before."

"Amen," said a woman.

"I was one of those guys who floated through life, getting the things he wanted, but not really deserving it," said Chino. "A lot of it was luck. Lots and lots of luck. But hey, when things are going your way, you don't question it. You just go with it. So that's what I did for a long time. I got married young to a beautiful woman who was way out of my league." His voice caught. "Her name was Aliesha. She was a good woman. She was... *the best*. And we had two beautiful kids." He looked up, looking into his peers' faces.

"Everyone says they have beautiful kids, but that's not true." There were some chuckles. "God knows I've seen some ugly-ass babies in my day."

"Amen," said someone else.

"But these kids were gorgeous. I've never been a big believer in God, but looking at the perfection of those kids... If there was a God, they were proof. Tyrese was the oldest. Tyrese was my little man. He looked up to me, wanted to be like me." Chino could feel the teardrop sitting in the bottom of his eye, wavering there. "Can you believe that? I sure couldn't." The tear fell, snaking its way down his cheek and into his beard. "Someone wanted to be like *me*? It never made sense, but it made me proud. It was just one more thing I didn't deserve. Then, a couple years after Tyrese was born, we had a little girl. Her name was Kailee. I'll be damned if she wasn't drop dead gorgeous like her mama." He sat there, smiling like a fool, staring at nothing for a moment.

His face went slack. "For a minute, we had the perfect life. We were happy. I would look at Aliesha and those kids and my heart would skip a beat. I was so happy. So... *proud*."

There were tears streaming down his face now, and he looked at the other alcoholics. He started to nod in a defiant manner. "But you know, it didn't last." There was anger in his voice now. "Just like everything good I had ever had..."

Chino snapped his fingers in front of his face.

"Gone," he said. "Just like that, they were gone. All three of 'em. Dead. Killed in a car accident by some fuckin' idiot who swerved into their lane." His voice cracked. He was looking down now, trying to regain his composure. "In the blink of an eye, my whole family was gone." He smiled a half-smile. "So then I made a new friend. His name was Jack Daniels. You mighta heard of him? Good guy, from Tennessee. And old Jack and me, we became real, *real* good friends. Inseparable. No matter what happened, who came or who went, Jack was there. He was my only friend."

He considered this, tilting his head at a realization. "Well, there was one other friend. But he never really lectured me about my drinking. Not at first. Then, once he did, he said it less and less. He figured it was too late for me, so he gave up. He was a realist. He knew the reality."

"What reality?" asked a young girl, maybe twenty-one, twenty-two.

"The reality that very few of us ever really change. We hate to admit that here." He looked at their smiles falling away. "A show of hands...

How many of you have relapsed a time or ten since you first vowed to stop drinking?" All the alcoholics looked around, unsure what to do. None of them raised their hands.

"It's not your fault," said Chino. "It's our nature. As people. It's who we are. So the reality that old Dobbs knew..." He looked up to clarify. "That was my friend, Dobbs... The reality was that I wasn't gonna change. And I didn't think I would change. I *shouldn't* have changed.

"I never woulda changed if I hadn't met Ericka," he said. "She changed everything. She saved my life. No two ways about it. And I wasn't worthy of her any more than I'd been worthy of Aliesha. But you know what? I wanted to *earn* this. Even after sobering up—she insisted on that, by the way—I still can't say that I've earned her, but I'm doin' my best."

"How bad was your alcoholism, my brother?" asked an old black man.

"It coulda been better, coulda been worse. I woke up lyin' outside in random places a few times, but that's par for the course. But it was bad enough. I was killin' myself. There were days where I didn't even eat. I just drank. And it had started affecting my work."

"What kinda work?" asked a cute little blonde.

"I was a consultant," he said. "But I drank all day, and it was fuckin' things up. In little ways at first, but then..." He looked at the table, chuckling to himself, thinking of Ericka. "Then I made a huge fuck up. It shoulda been the biggest fuck up of my life. But you know? It wasn't. My decision-making was faulty, but somehow it worked out. I lost my job and changed professions. That was tough. But none of that mattered. You know what did?"

He looked around the table at the faces watching him with rapt attention.

"Ericka mattered," he said. "She became my world. And suddenly, I was in a relationship again."

He stared down at the table, his eyes misting up.

"But it was hard. I realized I was an alcoholic. I mean, I knew I drank too much, but I didn't think I was a real, bonafide alcoholic. But I was. Ericka made me see." He looked up, his eyes wide now. "She made that painfully apparent. It mighta been lost on me, but it wasn't lost on her. She hated my drinking from the get-go, but it wasn't a huge issue at first. I don't know when it changed, " he said, pondering it for a moment. Then he looked up. "I take that back. It was the night we were lying in bed together and I pissed the bed. She woke up and wondered why the bed was wet. That didn't go over very well."

An older man to his left chuckled lightly.

"So I started coming here," Chino said.

"I fell off the horse a few times, but I got back up and got on that fucker. Not because I wanted to, but because she made me. Even if I didn't wanna get sober, I wanted her. So I kept comin'." He held up the coin again. "Today is a new day, and I'm extremely grateful for this new life I've found."

The room applauded.

After the meeting, after everyone had said the Lord's prayer and chanted "keep coming back, it works," Chino went to the coffee pot and poured himself a cup of Joe. He sat the pot down and turned, finding himself face-to-face with Ted.

"I'm proud of you, Chino."

Chino smiled. "You were a big part of this."

"I got another guy I'd like to introduce you to."

"Another customer?"

"Yeah. Fella's name is Carl."

SEVENTEEN

Chino was sitting on a park bench, listening to Carl tell his life story. The old man had taught high school sociology for thirty years. Had a couple kids who didn't speak to him. One even changed her last name to the name of her stepfather. His wife, his second, had been dust in the ground for a couple decades, and now Carl had been diagnosed with brain cancer. It was a shit life to be sure, and Chino didn't blame the guy for wanting to end it.

Carl looked at him. "Let's talk about the price."

"Nothin' to talk about," said Chino. "I told you. Sixty thousand, not a penny less."

Carl nodded, looking pained. Chino didn't

know if it was the price or the cancer. "I got it," said Carl.

"We good then?"

"Fine," he said. "Sixty grand."

"I'm gonna need the money upfront. Obviously I don't do payment plans for this sorta thing."

"I'd guess not." He reached into his jacket pocket and fished out a big thick envelope, handing it to over.

"What now?" Carl asked.

"You know the deal. We go our separate ways, I put you down. Closing credits."

"You'll kill me tonight?" asked Carl, sounding startled.

"Not tonight. Sometime in the next week or so."

"Why not tonight?"

"That's not how I do it. I've got my methods." This was a lie. Chino had only assisted five other people with their deaths, all over the past six months, and he still didn't know what he was doing. But he was figuring it out as he went. The pay was far less than what he'd made working for Cocoa, but it put food on the table and allowed him to scratch that itch—the desire to punch somebody's ticket every now and then.

"Well," said the old man, "do I get to choose how I die?"

"No."

"What if there's a specific way I wanna go out?"

"Then you're shit outta luck." Chino stared at him. "Or you find someone else. I'm sure there are a thousand junkies in this city who'd be glad to snuff you for a hundred bucks and bottle of vodka. Hell, some of 'em would probably do it just for the vodka."

"You think?"

"You know any junkies?"

"Not that I know of," said Carl.

"They're messy as fuck. I mean, they're junkies. They fuck up everything their grubby little hands touch. Do you really wanna entrust your death to some dirty meth-head who hasn't slept in a week?"

Carl just stared at him.

"You do that, you're likely to end up a fuckin' cucumber sittin' in the hospital the rest of your life. You don't ever trust a junkie with nothin', and I mean *nothin'*, but especially not this."

"You've done this a few times?"

"What do you want, a resume?"

"You got one?"

"I've done this. You know I have."

Carl looked down at the ground, nodding. "Ted says you killed his wife perfectly. Put her out of her misery." Carl looked at him again. "You remember her?"

"I do."

"You put a bullet through her heart, made it look like a car-jacker. That what you're gonna do to me?"

Chino shrugged. "You never know."

"Well, what *do* I know?"

"You know I'm gonna do the job, and I'm gonna do it right. I'm a pro, not some idiot who's gonna fuck it up and leave you half-dead or in a coma. With me, you're as good as dead, Carl."

The old man stared at him. "Can I ask you something?"

"Sure."

"Do you think there's an afterlife?"

"Does it matter what I think?"

"Not really," said Carl. "I was just wondering." He sat there silently, staring down for a moment. Then he looked at Chino. "Can I tell you something I've never told anyone?"

"It's your dime."

"I killed a man once."

"Yeah?"

Carl nodded. "I sure as shit did."

"In war?"

"Nah, it wasn't war. There was this guy I worked with. Math teacher named Chester. A real sonofabitch from the word go. This guy gave sonsofbitches a bad name. But worst of all, he used to whistle all the time. And man, I *hated* that. Hated it more than I can possibly express to you."

"So you killed him?"

"Well," said Carl. "He ain't whistlin' now."

Chino smiled. "How'd you do it?"

"One Saturday when he came over to watch the Sooners, I stabbed him. Used an old rusty pocket knife my daddy gave me when I was a kid. Stabbed him right in his eye."

He looked at Chino.

"How 'bout you?," he asked. "How many people you kill?"

"More than there's white bitches in Starbucks."

"That many?"

Chino shrugged. "It's what I do. So, did you write down all the stuff I asked you to? Your address and routine?"

"I did," said Carl, reaching into his jacket. This time he produced a folded piece of paper. Chino took it and looked at it.

"It all there?" asked Carl. "Everything you need?"

"Plenty."

"I got three questions."

"Okay. I'll give you three answers."

"Will I see it coming?"

"No," said Chino. "I promise you that. You'll just be livin' your life, goin' about your day, and then *bam!*, you'll be dead." He snapped his fingers. "Just like that."

"So you'll be quiet?"

"As quiet as God during the holocaust."

Carl stared at him, blinking.

"Then I'll be dead?"

"Deader than Lennon."

"John or Vladimir?"

"Take your pick."

Carl nodded, smiling. "Good. Then I'll get to see my wife in heaven."

"I hope that's true. What else?"

"You know how I killed Chester?"

"The guy you stabbed in the eye?"

"Will you promise not to kill me that way?"

Chino grinned. "I don't even have a pocket knife."

Carl smiled, reaching his hand out for Chino to shake. Chino stared at it for a moment. Carl's eyes locked with his, and Chino shook his hand. "I wanna thank you for this," said Carl. "I've lived a good life, but I'm ready. Thank you for helping me."

"Glad I could help."

"One last question."

"Ask away."

"I hope this doesn't offend you."

"I don't get offended."

"What happened to your ear?"

This caught Chino offguard. "That's a story for another day."

"I don't have another day."

"You might have a couple."

"You're not gonna tell me?"

"Some dickhead chewed it off in a fight."

"Did you kill him?"

"No," said Chino. "He was the one that got away."

"You regret that?"

"Every day of my life."

Chino stood. Carl looked up and asked, "This'll be the last time we meet?"

"The last you'll know about."

EIGHTEEN

THEY WERE SITTING at Ericka's favorite table inside her favorite restaurant. Chino was watching her speak, admiring her beauty. She was telling him about her friend Kimmie fighting with her piece of shit boyfriend, but Chino didn't wasn't listening. He just watched her, completely enraptured. He was as much in love —probably more so—as he'd been when they'd first met.

"I love you," he interrupted.

She blinked. "Where did that come from?"

"It's true."

"I love you, too."

"I know you do."

"So you're saying you don't wanna hear about Kimmie and Jake?"

"I'm just sayin' I love you. I don't give a fuck about Kimmie or Jake."

"Then what *do* you care about?"

"Just you."

She smiled, both of them staring at one another with goofy, lovey-dovey smiles on their faces.

"I don't know what I woulda done if I hadn't met you," he said. "Who knows where I'd be."

"Well, I know where I'd be."

"Where's that?" he asked.

"In the ground. If Cocoa had hired anyone else, I doubt they woulda fallen in love with me."

Chino grinned. "Maybe the other guy woulda fallen in love, too."

She smirked. "How often does that happen?"

"You're pretty lovable."

"Well, what if she'd sent a woman?"

"Same effect. That's how beautiful you are."

"The beauty that sunk a thousand ships?"

"You coulda turned her lesbian."

She grinned. "What if she already was?"

"Then it's a done deal," he said. "If she'd been a lesbian, we wouldn't be sittin' here. You'd be here with Candace."

"That's her name?"

"I just decided."

"You still make me laugh, even now after all this time."

"Let's not forget, I was a comedian."

She made a smart-ass expression. "But were you though? Were you *really*?"

"Of course I was."

"You stood up and told jokes, but were they *funny*?"

"You never saw me. I was almost as good a comic as I was a hitter."

"Well," she said, smiling. "You let me live, which makes you a pretty crappy hitter. So, if you were *almost* as good a comic..."

"What?"

"You sucked."

Chino grabbed a slice of bread, dabbing it in oil.

"I'm glad I married you," she said.

Chino had bread in his mouth, so he spoke through a mouthful of food. "I'm glad you married me, too."

"Where do you think you'd be today if you hadn't met me?"

"I told them at AA that I'd be dead if I hadn't met you."

"You think that's true?"

"Nah," said Chino. "I'm too big a bastard to

die. I'd probably still be alive, bustin' caps in people's asses by day, lyin' drunk and passed out in ditches by night."

She nodded. "That sounds about right."

"Why'd you marry me, Ericka?"

"I liked you. Even before you said you were gonna kill me."

"That was the line that won you over."

She laughed. "'I'm gonna kill you' is a line every girl dreams of hearing."

"I got a way with words."

"I knew you were a good guy and that you'd treat me right."

"Anything else?"

She shrugged. "You were cute."

"Even with my gut?"

"We got rid of that, didn't we?"

"Those were your rules," he said. "Stop drinkin' and lose the gut.'"

"What if I'd broken them?"

"Then I'd be here with Candace."

"I gotta kill that bitch."

She grinned. "Candace is a better hitter than you."

"Your daddy woulda been happier if you were with Candace."

"This is true," she said. "He doesn't love the gay thing, but he woulda taken it over you."

"How's he doin' lately?"

He was referring to the injury Cocoa's goons had inflicted upon her father, which had left him wheelchair-bound.

"Mom says he's gettin' around better these days."

"That's good."

"How's Dobbs?" she asked. "What's he been up to?"

"Same old shit."

"He still fishin'?"

Chino nodded. "He did what he had to. He had to get out the city after all that shit went down."

She nodded. "I get it."

"I haven't spoken to him in a week, but you know Dobbs. Dobbs don't change."

"Still runnin' around, fuckin' all them skanks?"

"Like I said, Dobbs don't change."

After dinner, they went to the movies. There wasn't anything playing that Ericka cared about, so Chino talked her into seeing a horror flick. It was about a hooker who was possessed by a demon and dismembers all her lovers. As they sat in the theater, he watched her hiding her eyes and screaming whenever something brutal was happening. The way she grabbed him and pulled him closer was the primary reason he took her to these.

After the movie, as they walked to the car, he asked, "What did you think of the movie?"

"You know I don't like that shit."

Chino chuckled. "It didn't give you any ideas, did it?"

"What kinda ideas?"

"You're not gonna dismember me, are you?"

"The night's still early. You never know."

Chino laughed. When they reached the car, she headed for the passenger side. She had only taken a couple steps when Chino said, "You forgot something."

She looked at him and smiled. She walked back to where he was standing and they embraced, kissing.

NINETEEN

BIGGIE'S "KICK IN THE DOOR" was playing inside the stolen Tahoe, and Chino was nodding his head appreciatively, waiting for Carl step out of the cafe. The cafe, Rick's Cafe American, was named after a location in *Casablanca*. "It's my favorite movie," Carl had said. "You know, I've probably seen it a hundred times." He'd asked Chino what movie he'd seen the most, to which Chino had answered *Goodfellas*.

"I go to that cafe every day," Carl said. "And every day, I have the same thing—soup and a sandwich. And I read. Mostly mysteries. But you know what I like most? I like to flirt with the pretty girls that work there. I read my book, and then, in between chapters, I flirt with 'em. I make jokes and ask 'em if they wanna take an old man home. But they never do."

As Chino sat in the Tahoe, wearing sunglasses—wearing them special for the occasion since he hated sunglasses—his cell phone rang. The ringtone was BBD's "Poison," telling him it was Ericka. He reached for the phone. As his gloved hand touched it, he kept his eyes on the cafe. He answered.

"Hey, pretty lady."

"What time will you be home?"

"Probably an hour and a half or so. I should be done here PDQ. But then I gotta dump the car and get the Beamer. What's up?"

"Well," she said. "I was thinkin'."

"Yeah?"

"I was thinkin', since you been a good boy and got your five-year sobriety chip, maybe you need a reward."

Chino smiled. "I think so too."

"I figured you would."

"What kinda reward you thinkin'?"

She said, "You know that fantasy you have..."

"The one where we pretend I'm a robber breakin' in?"

"One we haven't done before."

"The butt?"

"*No,*" she snapped. "Never that."

"Then what?"

"You said you wanted to have sex with me while I was wearin' my wedding dress."

"Tonight?"

"That okay?"

"Hell yeah."

Chino saw the door to the cafe open. "Hey," he said, letting the word hang. He saw that it was two old biddies, one with a poodle.

"Never mind," he said. "False alarm."

"So I get to keep you another minute?"

"You can keep me forever."

"You're not gonna cheat on me?"

"Never."

"Even if it was Halle Berry?"

"Well..."

She laughed. *"I knew it."*

"She's on my list," he said. "If it was Halle, I'd have no choice."

"I'm not even mad. It was me, *I'd* fuck Halle, too."

Chino chuckled.

"What you cookin' for dinner?" she asked.

"I'll grab somethin' on the way home. I mean, how am I gonna cook when we got all this wedding-dress fuckin' to do?"

She giggled. "You have a point."

"Girl, if you only knew."

"What's that supposed to mean?"

"It means I got a point for you."

"That a dick joke?"

"You know it is."

"You still ain't funny."

Chino was about to talk shit when he saw the cafe door open again. This time it was Carl.

"I gotta go to work," said Chino. "But I'll be home soon. Have that dress on when I get there."

Chino clicked off the phone and started the engine. He watched Carl, half a block down. Carl was standing there looking at a planter of flowers. Chino slowly edged the Tahoe out into the street, slightly faster than idle. Carl stepped forward, heading for the crosswalk.

Chino accelerated a bit, still moving slow. Carl looked both ways. Since Chino was in the far lane and moving slow as molasses, Carl stepped into the street. The moment his shoe touched the pavement, Chino gunned the Tahoe. Carl was about four steps out when he looked up and saw the Tahoe speeding towards him. Carl was mid-step in the second of four lanes. He stood there staring at Chino. Now there was a yellow car approaching from the other side. Chino's foot remained pressed all the way down, the Tahoe hurtling towards Carl and, inadvertently, towards the yellow car.

Carl just stood there, frozen, his eyes wide and his mouth open. He dropped his book. Chino was about ten feet from Carl now and was growing closer by the second. The yellow car was still twenty feet away and Chino knew he would miss it. In that last second before the Tahoe struck Carl, he and Chino locked eyes. In that briefest of moments, Chino felt bad for having lied to him. Carl *did* see him coming. He was standing there, motionless, when the Tahoe plowed into him. Chino heard the thump, felt the impact, and Carl shot up past the windshield and over the top.

Chino swerved to his right, making his way around the car. The car honked, and Chino wondered if it was to scold him for being in the lane or for murdering Carl. Chino didn't give a shit either way. He took a hard right at the next street, looking in his rearview. No one was following. He then hooked a hard left.

CHINO PULLED into the grocery store parking lot to switch cars. He was climbing into his Beamer when his cell phone rang again. The ringtone was "Can I Kick It?", so he knew it was Dobbs. Chino pulled off his gloves and started the car. He pulled out of the lot, letting Dobbs go to voicemail. He would call him back when he had some distance between himself and the Tahoe. Before he got half a block away, the phone rang again.

Chino picked it up and answered.

"What's crackin'?"

"Hello, Chino." He recognized the voice, but it wasn't Dobbs'.

"Cocoa," he said. "Where's Dobbs?"

Cocoa laughed, angering him.

"Where is he?!"

There was a pause. "Listen Chino." It was Dobbs now. "I ain't tell this bitch shit. But you better run. Both y'all. *Run!*"

Then he heard the deafening bark of a gunshot.

"Dobbs?!" cried Chino.

There was a pause, and Chino could hear rustling. His mind was reeling and he couldn't wrap his head around this. There were tears in his eyes.

"How you been, Chino?" asked Cocoa.

"Where's Dobbs?"

She laughed an evil laugh. "You'll see him soon enough."

"You bitch," he said. "Dobbs better be okay."

"He ain't okay. So what? You gonna come after me, Chino?"

Chino didn't know what to say. There was a long silence, Cocoa waiting for his response. Finally, he said, "Why *now*?"

"It's funnier this way. You're like the blind hooker—you never saw it comin'. I coulda killed you six years ago, but I let you live. Both you and that cunt wife of yours. But you know what? You were already dead. Both of you. I just let you believe you were still alive."

Chino thought of Ericka and became afraid. *"Ericka,"* he blurted, saying it to himself.

"You can't save her, Chino." She laughed. "You can't save anyone. Ask your pal Dobbs."

Chino hung up.

He stomped his foot on the gas and sped towards home. Maybe, just maybe, Ericka would be safe. But in his heart of hearts, he knew it was too late.

TWENTY

Rizzo and Cornbread were sitting in the car, staring at the house. Cornbread racked his pistol. "Let's get it on."

"This is Oklahoma," said Rizzo. "You can't go walkin' around with your gun out. These fuckin' hillbillies carry guns, sure, but they ain't packin' glocks with silencers. They got shotguns and shit. Muskets maybe. But not Glocks with silencers. You can't go runnin' around lookin' like Tommy fuckin' Rambo."

"I don't think Rambo's name was Tommy."

Rizzo stared at him. "What do you know, you cock-eyed fuck?"

"That ain't right. You ain't supposed to talk about a man's eyes."

"Says who?"

"It's a birth defect, Rizz."

"I wish you'd died at birth, you dumb bastard."

"You keep talkin' like that, I'm gonna put somethin' in your mouth."

This was music to Rizzo's ears. He loved confrontation, and he wanted to shoot this cock-eyed bastard. He'd wanted to put him in the ground ever since they'd met. "Oh yeah? What you gonna put in there?"

"Either my dick or my pistol. I ain't decided."

"You try that shit, you'll be a dead cock-eyed fuck."

"We got a job to do, man."

Both of them looked at Chino's house again. It was a nice place. Some suburban white bread *Leave It to Beaver* shit. Two stories, brick, with a Volvo in the drive.

"You sure this is it?" asked Rizzo.

"Why wouldn't it be?"

"I knew Chino. He had a different way about him. Thought he was black. Had a funny-lookin' ear. I dunno what was wrong with it. Looked like part of it was missin'. It's hard to picture him livin' out here in the sticks and drivin' a Volvo. Guy used to drive a Beamer."

"Beamers ain't shit."

"Better than a Volvo," said Rizzo. "Chino used to be a comedian. Can you believe that? The guy stood up in front of a room and told jokes. But you know what? I never thought he was funny."

"You saw his act?"

"No, but he was always crackin' jokes."

"I don't know shit about him."

"If you had, you'd have more reverence for the guy. He was really good. I didn't like him much, thought he was an asshole." He made a point to look at Cornbread. "But most guys in this line of work are."

"You sayin' I'm an asshole?"

"And then some."

"Get your head in the game, Rizz. We got a job to do."

"Let's go up and try the door."

"What if it's locked?"

"Then we'll 'round to the back."

"Why not just kick the door in?"

"This is one of them clean-cut neighborhoods. Probably a bunch of old white dudes who wear ugly khakis. Guys who get up at the crack of dawn and mow their lawns. People like that tend to notice things like cock-eyed Cubans carryin' Glocks and kickin' down doors."

Cornbread nodded.

They climbed out of the car and walked across the street.

"You stand at the edge of the house and keep watch," said Rizzo. "I'll go up and try the door." Cornbread nodded, and they went their separate ways. Rizzo tried the door, but it was locked.

Rizzo walked back towards Cornbread.

"You think she's in there?" Cornbread asked.

"How should I know? I got the same information you got."

Cornbread turned towards the backyard. Rizzo followed. There was a wooden privacy fence. As they approached the gate, Cornbread asked, "You think they got a dog back there?"

"Again, how would I know?"

Cornbread tried the gate, finding it locked. "What now?"

"Outta the way."

"You know how to unlock it?"

"I do." Rizzo stepped forward and kicked the gate hard, busting it open.

Chino was speeding through the city, running stop signs and red lights willy-nilly. Luckily, he didn't encounter any pedestrians. If he had, they woulda been dead pedestrians. Chino's mind was racing, and he was overcome with dread.

He'd tried to call Ericka twice, but his calls had gone straight to voicemail. He tried a third time. Same result—straight to voicemail.

His heart was pounding, and he was sweating profusely. Maybe Ericka was okay, he told himself. Maybe.

And then he heard the siren behind him. He looked in the rearview, seeing the flashing lights of a police cruiser.

Rizzo and Cornbread were in the backyard now. Cornbread motioned towards the swimming pool. "I always wanted a pool. How 'bout you? You got a pool?"

"Shut your cock-eyed ass up," Rizzo growled.

"Fuck you. You ain't the boss."

"I was workin' for Cocoa before you even stepped on that banana boat. I got seniority."

"There ain't no seniority. We're equals."

Rizzo swiveled and stuck his Glock in Cornbread's face, touching his nose with its tip. "Say that again. Just once. See what happens."

Cornbread was pissed but kept his mouth shut. Seeing he wasn't gonna say shit, Rizzo stepped onto the wooden deck. He approached the backdoor, Cornbread behind him. "This cocksucker's livin' like a king out here," said Rizzo.

"Just open the door."

They were at the sliding door now. The curtain was closed and they couldn't see in. Rizzo wrapped his fingers around the handle and slid the door to the left, stepping in through the curtain. When he emerged on the other side, he saw Ericka standing in a white wedding dress.

Chino pulled over. It was broad daylight on a fairly busy street, and the cop was taking his sweet time to get out his cruiser. *Dammit,* Chino thought. He really needed to get to Ericka. He would never forgive himself if she died. He looked in the mirror and saw the cop getting out. Chino rolled the window down as he watched the fat sunglasses-wearing cop saunter towards him.

"What can I do for you, officer?"

"You know how fast you was goin'?"

"I don't."

"Seventy in a forty."

Chino looked at him, feeling like he might bust out of his skin at any second. His heart was racing and he could hardly catch his breath. He had to get to Ericka.

"Lemme see your license and registration."

Chino didn't have time for this. When it came to Ericka, nothing was off the table. He would kill this cop to get to her. Chino's fingers were wrapped around the handle of his pistol. His finger was on the trigger. He was about to raise the gun when the cop got a call. The cop took it on a CB thing on his chest. Chino didn't know what they were talking about, but he was ready to kill the pig. Suddenly, the cop said, "I gotta go." The cop raced back to his vehicle, hopped in, and took off, sirens blaring.

Chino dropped the Beamer into drive and stomped on the gas.

TWENTY-ONE

WHEN CHINO SAW the black car, he knew it belonged to Cocoa's guys. Was he too late? Chino entered the driveway and drove the Beamer up into the yard, stopping in front of the porch. He got out, gun in hand. He was on the porch in seconds, trying the door. He stepped back and kicked it hard, breaking it open. The door shot back and struck the wall. Chino rushed in, gun up and ready. There was no one in the living room. He went into the hallway, checking the bedrooms. He then made his way through the house, heading towards the dining room. As he did, he could smell cigarette smoke. He could see the dining room table ahead, but no one was there. He brought his gun up before he rounded the corner to the kitchen.

The first thing he saw was blood. Everywhere.

The cigarette smoke was thick.

Shocked by what he saw, he stood there motionless.

He looked at Ericka, sitting in a dining room chair pulled into the kitchen, smoking a cigarette. She was wearing her white wedding dress, now splattered with blood. Chino looked down at her pretty feet, seeing the bodies of the two hitmen beside them.

Ericka just stared at him.

He said, "You don't smoke."

"We need to talk."

Chino looked at the bodies again. "I think you're right." He walked over to one of them. He pushed the guy's body over with his foot so he could see his face. His throat was cut from ear to ear. "Rizzo Rizzulo," Chino said. "I never liked him."

He looked at Ericka, trying to understand.

"You should sit," she said.

He was confused. His head was reeling. He looked around, seeing no place to sit.

Ericka nodded towards the dining room. "Grab a chair."

Chino dragged a chair into the kitchen, lifting it over the bodies. He sat down, staring at Ericka.

"What is all this?"

She was mid-drag. She pulled the cigarette from her lips and exhaled, blowing out smoke.

"Cocoa sent them," she said. "And I killed them."

"By yourself?"

"You see anybody else here?"

"And you smoke?"

She stared at him. *"That's what you're focusing on?"*

"You said you quit."

"Well, now I'm smoking again." She looked down at the bodies. "Extenuating circumstances."

"Where'd you get the smokes?"

"The cock-eyed Cuban," she said. "I hate Camels, but I wanted a smoke."

"So, what am I missing here?"

"When we met..."

"Yeah?"

"There mighta been some stuff I left out."

He stared at her in disbelief. Then he looked at the dead men again.

"I was mostly honest," she said. "Didn't lie about much."

"How about the butt stuff? Did you lie about that?"

She rolled her eyes. "Dammit, Chino."

He nodded. "You're right."

"Back in the city... I mighta killed a few people."

"What?!"

"It's not like you never did it."

There wasn't much he could say. "Okay," he said. "Explain it to me like I'm a five-year-old. Who did you kill?" He looked at the dead guys again. "Back in the city."

"I wouldn't call myself a serial killer, per se..."

"Per se?!" he said. *"What the hell, Ericka?"*

"We all got skeletons in our closets."

"Let me get this straight: *you were a serial killer?"*

"Not *really*. It was just a hobby. When I was a kid, I knew I was different. I always had a taste for it."

"For what?"

"Killing."

"Since you were a kid?"

"The first guy I killed was Mr. Tanner. He was my math teacher. Fucker took my virginity when I was in the eighth grade."

"You never told me."

"I didn't tell anyone. There was no need since I took care of it myself. The next year, after I'd gone on to high school, I watched his house a few days, studying him. Then, finally, I snuck out one night in the middle of the night and I went over to there and killed him."

"Really?"

Her eyes got big, and a grin spread across her face. "I killed the fuck outta him. I took this antique knife my Daddy had. It was an old Nazi knife, from World War II. He kept it on display in his study. So I took that knife, and I..." She grinned a devilish grin. "I gutted him. I cut him from his dick to his throat."

Chino sat there, listening in silence.

"After that, I didn't kill anybody until college," she said. "But I *felt* it. It was always there."

"What?"

"The itch. You know what I mean?"

Chino did. "I know that itch."

"You said you didn't enjoy you work."

He shrugged. "It was like readin'."

"How so?"

"Some people say they like readin', but they only like readin' what they wanna read. It's not as fun when it's an assignment."

"Killin's like that?"

"And I was burned out. But also, I didn't

wanna tell you I enjoyed killin' folks. I mean, who wants to be with someone who enjoys that?"

She smiled, pointing at herself. "This girl here."

"How many people have you killed?"

Ericka didn't skip a beat. "Twenty-three." She looked down at the two dead men. "Sorry. Twenty-*five*."

This aroused Chino.

"You killed twenty-three people in the city?"

"Not all in the city," she said. "I scattered 'em around. Killed 'em in different places. Different ways. I didn't want there to be similarities—anything that might give some bright boy cop the idea they were connected."

"That's what you told me to do. You said to kill all the old people in different ways so no one could connect 'em."

She tapped her forehead. "Experience."

"So how did you pick your victims?"

"Different ways," she said. "The ones I liked best were social justice murders."

"I don't follow."

"A few of 'em were bad people who'd done bad things. But the rest were just random."

"Wait," he said. "You killed *innocent* people?"

"Nobody's innocent, Chino."

He looked at her, trying to understand. "There's a code."

"In your world, yes. But this was *my world.* This was outside the lines. I don't feel good about it, but I didn't know what else to do. I needed that fix." She looked at him. "You're an alcoholic. You know what that's like."

"Tell me about the bad people. How did you know they were bad?"

"One was a cop. He lived in Massachusetts. He'd shot and killed an unarmed man named Trevor Thompson."

"What had Trevor Thompson done?"

"Nothing at all. The motherfucker had a burnt-out turn signal. Mighta mouthed off. I dunno. But he was unarmed, and there was a video of the cop shooting him in the back of the head."

"Maybe if you hadn't killed him, they woulda found him guilty and he'd have gone to jail."

"No," she said. "He'd already gone to court, and they found him innocent. The cop said he feared for his life."

"Have you killed anybody since we moved to Tulsa?"

She made an awkward expression, like a deer caught in headlights.

"What?" asked Chino.

"You remember that guy they found last year at Keystone Lake?"

Chino shook his head. "No."

"You remember," she said. "The guy who was missin' his head, arms, and legs."

"That was you?"

She nodded.

"What did he do?"

"He was a pedo. Raped little girls."

Chino stared at her.

"He was a teacher," she said.

"And he reminded you of the guy who hurt you."

"Mr. Tanner."

Chino looked at the dead guys on the floor again. "How'd you manage this?"

"They were arguing with each other," she said. When the one guy, Rizzo, had his head turned, I slashed his throat with a steak knife. Before the cock-eyed guy could move, I shot him with Rizzo's gun."

"Damn," said Chino, staring at her. "I've never been more attracted to you."

"I'm wearin' the dress."

He eyeballed it appreciatively. "It looks good."

"Even with blood on it?"

"*Especially* with blood on it."

"What do you wanna do?"

"I think you know."

"Where?"

"Right here," said Chino. "On the counter."

She paused, considering it. "What about the dead guys?"

Chino grinned. "They won't care."

Chino sat his pistol on the floor. They both stood. Chino embraced her and they kissed. He turned her body to the side and her ass was touching the cabinet. He lifted her onto the counter, and they kissed hard. She wrapped her legs around him, and he reached down between her legs. "You're not wearing panties."

She grabbed him and pulled him towards her. "Shut up and fuck me."

ACT THREE

TWENTY-TWO

COCOA WAS HIDING out in a little farmhouse two miles outside Dryden. It was her and some of her best guys. Her *consigliere*, Max, assured her she would be safe there, but she had doubts. She knew Chino and knew what kind of damage he was capable of.

She was sitting in a recliner, holding her new poodle, Dee Dee, talking on the phone with Max. Max had stayed behind to handle day-to-day operations.

"Everything's fine here," he said. "That fucker shows up, he's in for a rude awakening. I got half our guys staked out here. Besides, he's not gonna want me. It's you he wants."

"You ask around to see if anybody's heard anything?"

"Of course," he said.

Cocoa hated Max, and his smugness was even worse. He always sounded condescending. He was a mansplaining piece of shit. She should never have hired him, but she did. And she regretted it. As they spoke, she made a mental note to get rid of him when this Chino business was over.

"Nobody's heard a thing," said Max. "The guys we sent down to Tulsa—the ones after Rizzo and that cock-eyed fucker—haven't found anything. And I been callin' all our contacts. Like I said, nobody knows nothin'."

"Just keep your eyes peeled," said Cocoa. "You don't know Chino."

"I always heard he was good."

Cocoa laughed.

"What?" asked Max.

"Don't underestimate him. He's not good, he's *the best*. I've seen a lotta hitters come and go. The only other guy I ever heard of who was comparable was this guy from Chicago. They call him Saint Lewis. He's good. Maybe even better than Chino. But it's close. Both of 'em are gods in this world. Chino's a guy you don't fuck with."

"Then why did you?"

The question stung, but Max was right. Cocoa had been asking herself the same thing. But she didn't care to be questioned by an underling. "Don't worry about it, Maxy. You just keep your mouth shut and do your fuckin' job."

Max tried to backpedal, "I didn't mean..."

"Yes, you did. You meant that."

"No, I..."

"Max."

"Yeah?"

"Who's the boss?"

"Whaddaya mean?"

"Am I the boss, or are you the boss?"

"Come on," he said.

"Answer the question."

"You are."

"Then if I say you meant it, you meant it."

Silence.

Cocoa asked, "You hear me, Maxy?"

"I did."

"Then say it."

"Say what?"

"You meant I fucked up."

There was a pause. Max said, "I didn't..."

"Say the words, goddammit!"

"I meant you mighta made a mistake."

"Bullshit!" she screamed. *"Say what I told you to say. Say 'I meant you fucked up'!"*

Cocoa heard him gulp. "You fucked up."

"Say you think I'm stupid, Max."

"Please..."

"Say you think I'm a stupid bitch. Say you think I'm inferior to you. That you should be the boss."

"I don't wanna say that."

"Max."

"Please."

"I'm not gonna ask again. I say it again, you're gonna get hurt."

"Okay." Max gulped again. "I think you're..." His voice was wavering. "Stupid."

"And?"

"Inferior."

"And a bitch?"

He paused. "You want me to say that?"

"You think it. You might as well say it."

"I don't..."

"Jesus Christ, Max."

"Okay, damn. You're a bitch."

"A *stupid* bitch," she said.

"A stupid bitch."

"And who should be the boss?" Cocoa asked.

"I... I should be the boss."

"Good. Now you've said it. Let's get this shit straight right now, you little nickel dick cock-sucker. *I'm* the boss. The *only* boss. As far your ass is concerned, I'm God up here, and you will put no Gods before me. You understand that, Maxy? That's the deal. You don't like it, or you wanna talk shit and question me, feel free. And you'll find yourself chopped up in itty-bitty pieces at the bottom of the river."

"I'm sorry," Max said.

"You are."

"Cocoa, listen..."

She hung up.

After getting yelled at by Cocoa, Max looked at Jeremiah, his bodyguard. "The fellas outside?"

Jeremiah nodded.

"Send 'em in."

The big, muscular, former welterweight nodded and left. As Max waited for him to return, he sat there fuming about the way Cocoa treated him. Thinking about it made him angry. He looked down at the ink pen he was holding, staring at it for a moment before hurling it across the room. The door opened, and Jeremiah led the two guys, Joe Woody and Jim Bob, in.

Max looked at them and said, "Have a seat, guys." He looked at Jeremiah. "Jerry, would you wait outside?" The bodyguard nodded and left, closing the door behind him.

Max looked at them, sizing them up. Joe Woody was older—a red-haired guy nearing sixty. He'd been around since before Cocoa. He'd been a knockaround guy for years before working as a hitter. He was decent. Not the best, but pretty good. Second string. But that's where they were now that Chino had killed Rizzo and Cornbread. And Jim Bob was a different kinda guy. He looked like a lumberjack. Big corn-fed redneck with a bushy blonde beard.

"You know what?" Max said to Jim Bob.

"What?"

"You look like Grizzly Adams."

Jim Bob looked puzzled. "I dunno who that is. He one of Carmine's guys?"

Max looked at Joe Woody. "You believe this shit? Fuckin' guy don't know who Grizzly Adams is."

"He's young," said Joe Woody. "I'm forty-two, and I don't even remember that."

"You're stupid too," said Max. He looked at Jim Bob. "From now on, you're Grizzly Adams."

Jim Bob was confused. He looked at Joe Woody to see if he should be offended. Joe Woody looked at him and said, "Forget about it."

The big lunk nodded and shrugged, and that was that.

"You guys are gonna go to Dobbs' funeral and hang back, watch for Chino," said Max. "Then, when you see him, *blam!* You take 'im out."

"At the funeral?" asked Jim Bob.

"Right there. We can't play around with this guy."

"Can I interject something?" said Joe Woody.

"Interject away."

"Chino ain't that stupid. No way in hell he goes anywhere near that funeral."

Max tapped his forehead. "I'm smarter than you, Joe."

Joe Woody and Jim Bob exchanged glances.

"If I say jump, you fuckin' jump."

Joe Woody shrugged. "Whatever you say, pal."

"You're damn right."

"But he ain't gonna be there," Joe Woody repeated.

Max glared at him. "He'll be wherever the fuck I say he'll be."

Jim Bob chuckled at this, and Max turned his gaze towards him. "You think that's funny, farm boy?"

Jim Bob looked at him dumbly, considering it. "Kinda."

Max stared at him for a moment and then just shook his head. "So you two go out to the cemetery, and you wait for Chino. But you split up. We can't afford to lose both of you."

"But you can lose one?" asked Joe Woody.

"You moronic cocksuckers do a good job, and we won't have to worry about it."

"He ain't gonna be there anyway."

Max glared at him. "You and me, we're gonna go 'round and 'round one of these days."

"I can't wait."

Max looked at Jim Bob. "You see Chino, what are you gonna do?"

"I'm gonna put a bullet in him."

"Multiple bullets," said Max.

Jim Bob nodded, grinning. "I'll fill that sonofabitch with more holes than a gloryhole porno booth."

TWENTY-THREE

Joe Woody was sitting in the Bonneville with his window down, smoking a cigarette. He was watching the graveside service from a distance. He looked around, seeing all kinds of wiseguys, but no Chino. The radio was on and he was listening to NPR. *Fresh Air* was on and they were talking with a woman who'd written a book about George W. Bush.

Joe Woody reached into his jacket and pulled out his flask. He unscrewed the lid and looked at the service, raising the flask to salute Dobbs. He'd never really liked Dobbs, but he'd respected him. Dobbs was a standup guy. He'd hated having to kill him. But that was the job. Dobbs knew that as well as anyone. Dobbs was a legend. Not quite as much as Chino, but he was respected by every wiseguy who'd ever known him (including the ones he'd clipped).

"Salute!" Joe Woody said, taking a swig.

He was screwing the lid back on when he heard the backseat door open. Before he could react, he felt the silencer touch the back of his head.

"Who's there?" he asked.

"You know," said the voice.

Joe Woody grinned. "Chino Genetti, half-eared comedian."

"It's funny. I killed more guys than you've known your whole life, and yet all anyone ever mentions is the comedian thing."

"You gonna kill me?"

"Maybe, maybe not."

Joe Woody turned his head to the side. *"Maybe not?"*

"You tell me what I wanna know, maybe I let you live. Maybe you won't be the second body goin' in the ground today."

"I don't believe you," said Joe Woody.

"Either way, it's all the same."

"How's that?"

"Way I see it, you got two options."

"Okay, what's the first?"

"You tell me what I wanna know," said Chino.

"The second?"

"You eat a bullet."

Joe Woody considered this for a moment. Then he said, "Chino?"

"Yeah?"

"Tell me a joke, seein' how you're so funny. I never heard you tell a joke."

"It don't work that way, Joe."

"Then how's it work?"

"It's hard to just come up with shit on the spot."

"Sounds like a cop out."

"Okay," Chino said. "There's this Chinaman..."

"That shit ain't P.C.," said Joe Woody. "You ain't supposed to say Chinaman no more. Get with the times, man. Chinaman is out. You're supposed to say Asian man. You can't even say *Oriental* man, let alone chink or any of that."

"You wanna hear the joke or not?"

Joe Woody shrugged.

"Okay," said Chino. "This Chinaman—"

"Asian man."

"Okay. This Asian man calls his boss. He says, 'Me no work today, me sick.' The boss says, 'Try what I do. Maybe that'll help. I go fuck my wife in the ass for two hours and then I'm good as new. Try that.' The Asian man says okay. Two hours later he calls back and says, 'Okay, I try it. It work. You sure got a nice house.'"

Joe Woody chuckled. "I guess it's true what they say," he said.

"What's that?"

"You were a piss-poor comic."

"Well, you're a piss-poor hitter. I can't believe they gave you this job. You were a fuckin' lackey back when I knew you. A good for nothin' bum."

"You think I'm a bad hitter?"

"I'm in the backseat with a gun to your head."

Joe Woody shrugged. "True enough."

"Cocoa wouldn't send just one swingin' dick, and if she did, I'd hope to hell she'd know enough to send someone better than you," said Chino. "Who else is here?"

"Go fuck yourself, funny man."

Chino pressed the silencer against Joe Woody's head.

"If the next sentence outta your mouth is anything other than what I'm askin', you die. Consider your words carefully, Joe."

"Okay. There's another fella. Redneck guy. Blonde *Hee-Haw*-lookin' fucker named Jim

Bob."

"Jim Bob? Is that real?"

"I know. It sounds like a stereotype."

"Where'd they find him? Cocoa hirin' hitters off Craigslist?"

"Hell if I know."

"Blonde guy, huh?"

"Got a big bushy beard. Max says he looks like Grizzly Adams, but I don't know who that is."

"Who's Max?"

"He's Cocoa's *consigliere*. Real asshole."

"Yeah?"

"*Oh yeah.* Think of the biggest asshole you ever seen and then multiply that by a thousand. And then, maybe...you *almost* got Max. I'm tellin' ya, he's the king of the douchebags."

"He been around long?"

"A few years, I think."

"Huh," said Chino. "I'm assuming Cocoa is hiding somewhere."

"You think you're that tough, Chino? Tough enough that Cocoa's holed up somewhere?"

"You and I both know it's true," said Chino. "Where's she at?"

Joe Woody looked out the window and sighed. "I tell you that, I'm a dead man."

"If you *don't* tell me, you're a dead man."

Joe Woody sat there for a long moment, staring out the window. Finally, he said, "You wanna hear a joke, Chino?"

"Not really."

"Humor me, Chino. Just one."

"Okay."

"It's a riddle."

Chino remained silent.

"Who shot your pal Dobbs, right in his nigger face?"

Chino became angry immediately. "*Who?*"

Joe Woody chuckled. "I did. How you like that, funny guy?"

Chino pushed the tip of the silencer hard against the man's head, and Joe Woody closed his eyes.

"I'm not gonna kill you, asshole," said Chino. "I'm gonna take you somewhere and make you suffer."

"What? You gonna tell me some more of your jokes?"

"I'm gonna hurt you *real* bad, Joe. I'm gonna hurt you so bad your mama's gonna feel it."

"My mama's dead, Chino."

"Maybe you'll see her soon."

"Only if that bitch is in hell," said Joe Woody.

"Well, your mama—" He stopped in mid-sentence when Joe Woody yelped and Chino saw the arm coming through the window. As Joe Woody made a gurgling sound, Chino realized what was happening. Ericka was standing outside with her hand in the window, shoving a knife into Joe Woody's temple. Chino sat there, stunned. Joe Woody didn't die immediately. It took him a minute or so, his body twitching and convulsing. Ericka let out a guttural growl as she twisted the blade inside Joe Woody's head, and he finally stopped moving.

Ericka pulled the knife out and leaned down, looking at Chino through the window. "Hey baby," she said.

"What the hell, Ericka?"

"Just kill him and be done with it."

"We were talkin', Ericka!"

"About what? Fantasy football?"

"I was tryin' to find out where Cocoa is."

"Did you get anything?"

"No, Ericka. You killed the fuckin' guy before I could get it outta him."

Ericka shrugged. "Maybe talk faster next time."

Chino climbed out of the car. "There's a second guy here," he said. "We need to find him. Maybe get somethin' out of him."

"We won't," said Ericka.

"What do you mean?"

"I already killed him."

Chino stared at her. "You killed him? *When?*"

"While you were chit-chattin' with this fucker."

"How'd you spot him?"

"It was pretty easy. I could tell just by lookin' at him."

"How?"

"He looked like a hitman."

"He looked like me?"

"Well, no," she said. "But he still looked like a hitman."

"Guess what, Ericka? Half the people at this funeral are probably hitmen. Dobbs was a hitter. These are his friends. You're sure you killed the right guy?"

She looked irritated. "Of course."

"What did he look like?"

"Black guy. Muscular. Looked like Hawk from *Spencer for Hire*."

"You killed him?"

"Sure did," she said.

"You killed the wrong guy," said Chino. "The guy we're lookin' for is a big blonde fucker with a beard."

Ericka shrugged. "I guess I did kill the wrong guy."

"Dammit, baby. You gotta stop killin' innocent people."

"Nobody's innocent."

TWENTY-FOUR

Max didn't wanna call Cocoa, but he saw no choice. He was sitting at her desk, feeling frustrated and angry. He looked at Jeremiah, sitting there staring at him.

"You alright, Boss?" asked Jeremiah.

"Mind your own fuckin' business."

"Sorry, Boss." Jeremiah was trying to look happy, but Max knew he wasn't. But fuck him. Fuck everybody. Most of all, fuck Cocoa. He looked at Jeremiah again. "Hey Jerry, I need you to go outside for a minute. Have a smoke, why don't you?"

"I don't smoke."

"Then smoke a joint. Isn't that what you people do?"

Jeremiah glared at him, saying nothing. The look on his face told Max he would have beat the shit out of him under different circumstances. Max pointed towards the door. "Just go do whatever it is you do. I need to call Cocoa." Jeremiah smirked, letting Max know he'd overheard him getting dressed down. This irritated Max even more, but he let it go. Once Jeremiah was gone, Max picked up the cell phone and hit the button.

A moment later, Cocoa answered. "*What?*"

That was a shitty way to answer, he thought.

"It's about the funeral."

"How'd it go?"

"Not as well as we'd hoped."

"Goddammit. They fuck it up?"

"Yeah."

"Chino?"

"I'm assuming it was Chino but can't verify it. Somebody stabbed Joe Woody in the head."

"At the funeral?" asked Cocoa.

"That's what I'm sayin'."

"You talkin' back to me?" There was a sharpness to her voice, and Max knew he'd said the wrong thing again.

"No, Cocoa."

"You don't get to call me Cocoa anymore."

"I've always called you Cocoa."

"Your Cocoa rights have been revoked. From

now on you call me boss. 'Cause that's what I am. I'm the fuckin' boss, and you're the fuckin'... *Nothin'*. That's what you are. Nothin'. You're dog shit off the bottom of my heels. Not even that. You're less than dog shit."

This irked him. "What's less than dog shit?"

"You, motherfucker."

"Then why'd you hire me?"

"We all make mistakes."

"I was a mistake?"

"Of course you were a mistake. Ask your parents."

"That's a terrible thing to say."

"Fuck you, Maxy. I don't give a rat's ass what you think. Your ass ain't worth five bucks, so you best shut up before I make change."

Max sat there, angry, but said nothing.

"Tell me about the funeral," she said.

"I already did."

"Let's run through this. Joe Woody's dead, right?"

"Like I said."

"Did anybody *see* Chino?"

"No. Apparently he was in and out like a fuckin' ninja."

"What about hillbilly boy? What did he do?"

"Jim Bob?"

"Yeah, the cracker."

"He didn't see nothin'," said Max. "Said he was standin' in the cemetery, watchin' the funeral. Didn't see a thing."

"I told you not to hire that inbred sonofabitch."

"He came with references."

"Workin' for Missouri meth dealers don't count."

Max kept his mouth shut.

"I'm gonna remember this," she said.

"What?"

"That you failed me."

"I failed you?"

"You *always* fail me. But that's a conversation for another day. Right now what I wanna talk about is Billy Bob Joe Jim Bob or whatever the fuck his name is."

"Jim Bob."

"Cracker-ass cracker."

"You want me to talk to him?"

"No," she said. "I want you to kill him."

"That's extreme."

"Just do what I say and kill his ass."

Max nodded, realizing he needed to go along with this. He was already in enough hot water with her. "Okay," he said. "Any preference on who and how?"

"I want you to do it."

"*Me?*"

"Do I stutter, motherfucker?"

"No. But I don't kill people."

"You're a pussy. We gotta toughen you up, Max."

"So *I* kill him?"

"Yep."

He sighed. "Okay, you got any preference about how I do it?"

"Ice pick city," she said.

"Ice picks?"

"Yes, Maxy."

"In his eyes?"

"There a different way?"

"I heard of a guy stickin' an ice pick in a man's dickhole once."

"You can do that too if you want. I don't care. But definitely the eyes."

Max nodded. "I can do that."

"You sure?"

"Sure, I'm sure."

"You just make sure it's you and not somebody else. I find out you had somebody else do it, you'll end up with ice picks in your eyes too. You understand? You bitch out and make somebody else do it, I'll make sure you disappear and nobody ever finds the pieces."

Max remained silent.

"We clear on this?"

"Yes, Cocoa." He corrected himself. "*Boss.* I mean yes, *Boss.*"

She hung up.

JIM BOB WAS SITTING on the toilet in his apartment taking a shit when he heard the front door bust in. He was mid-shit, so he couldn't move. He didn't even have his gun with him.

"Is somebody here?" he asked.

No answer.

"I'll fuck you up!" he yelled. *"I mean it. I got a gun in here!"*

A moment later, a couple low-level goons he knew, Parker and some Puerto Rican dude whose name he couldn't remember, appeared in the doorway. Both had their pistols trained on him.

The Puerto Rican held his nose. "Goddamn, Jim Bob," he said. "It smells like somethin' done climbed up your ass and died."

"What do you guys want?"

"We're supposed to take you in," said Parker.

"Cocoa send you?"

"I don't know the specifics," said Parker. "All I know is Max called and told us to bring you in."

"For what?"

"How the fuck do we know?" asked the Puerto Rican. "We just do what we're told. That's above our pay grade."

Parker looked at Jim Bob. "How 'bout you? Did you do what *you* were told?"

Jim Bob, still shitting, bit his lip. "I think I did."

"Then you should be fine," said Parker.

"You got nothin' to worry about as long as you've done what you were told to do," said the Puerto Rican.

"So we gotta go *now?*" asked Jim Bob.

"Five minutes ago," said Parker.

"Can you just give me a few minutes to finish? I got half a shit hangin' out my ass."

Parker and the Puerto Rican laughed, looking at each other.

"You better break that turd in half," said Parker.

"We ain't got time for you to finish," said the Puerto Rican.

Jim Bob was distressed now. "I can't go with half a turd hangin' out."

The Puerto Rican pointed his gun at him. "Mr. .45 says otherwise. He says you can."

Parker chuckled. "Get your big ass up off the toilet."

"But—"

"Ain't no buts," said the Puerto Rican. "'Cept your butt, shitty as it is."

The two goons laughed.

Jim Bob's face was red. "This is fucked up, guys."

"You'll be alright," said Parker.

"Why can't I finish my shit? Are we really in that big a hurry?"

Parker was laughing when the Puerto Rican turned to him. "Maybe we should let him finish. What's it gonna hurt? We're in my Caddy, and I don't want this motherfucker smellin' like shit in there. It's still got that new car smell."

"What?" asked Parker, grinning. "You don't want it to have Jim Bob shit smell?"

"Hard pass," said the Puerto Rican.

Parker shrugged. He looked at Jim Bob. "Alright, Jethro, you got five minutes. You go ahead and crank that shit out quick so we can go. I'm gonna time you."

The Puerto Rican looked at Parker. "You got a watch?"

"No," said Parker.

"How 'bout a cell phone?"

Parker shook his head. "Left it in the car. You?"

"Same," said the Puerto Rican.

"Okay," said Parker, staring at Jim Bob. "Just

fuckin' hurry. If it feels like it's longer than five minutes, we're gonna go, shit in or shit out."

An hour later, Jim Bob was tied to an office chair in Cocoa's office. Max and Jeremiah were standing over him.

"You done fucked up," said Max.

"I didn't do nothin'," said Jim Bob.

Max shrugged. "Therein lies the problem. You were supposed to kill Chino. But you didn't see the guy, even though he killed your partner a hundred feet away. That's a bad look, man. Put yourself in Cocoa's shoes, what would you do?"

"I'd tell me to do better next time."

Jeremiah chuckled. Max looked over at him.

"You made Jerry chuckle," said Max. "I ain't never seen this nigger chuckle once. Most the time the motherfucker don't even talk. But that's how far off the mark you are. Givin' second chances ain't in Cocoa's vocabulary. She don't know them words. She ain't in the business of givin' second chances."

"I did my best," pleaded Jim Bob. "It's not my fault."

Max looked at Jeremiah. "What you think?"

"I don't know."

"Would you let him live?"

Jeremiah shrugged.

Max turned back towards Jim Bob. "Don't matter. It's all woulda, coulda, shoulda at this point. Your fate is sealed. Cocoa wants you in a box. So it's written, so it shall be done."

Jim Bob started to beg. Max looked over at Jeremiah. "Put a gag in his mouth."

"I ain't got no cloth to gag him with."

"Hmmm," said Max, thinking.

"Gimme a second chance," said Jim Bob. "Tell her I'm sorry."

Max looked at Jeremiah. "I got it. There's a rag in the bathroom. I use it to wipe my dick off after I jerk off. We can stick that in his mouth."

"Fuck that!" said Jim Bob.

Jeremiah was staring at Max. "This is where I draw the line, Boss. You wanna put a cum rag in this dude's mouth, you doin' it yourself. I ain't tryin' to touch nobody's cum rag."

"Jesus Christ!" yelled Jim Bob. *"You motherfuckers better let me go!"*

Max stared at Jeremiah, wanting to scold him for insubordination, but seeing his point. "Okay," he said. "I'll get the rag. You shut this cocksucker up." As Max headed towards the bathroom, he heard Jeremiah clock Jim Bob in the face. Max went in and grabbed the crusty rag sitting on the back of the toilet. He grabbed it and returned to Jeremiah and Jim Bob.

Max held up the rag. "This fucker's so stiff I can hold it sideways and it'll look like a flag, flyin' in the wind."

Max and Jeremiah chuckled. Jim Bob didn't.

"Please, no," pleaded Jim Bob, crying now.

"It's so stiff I figured it would get up and walk away sometime," Max said. "Catholics believe jerkin' off is murder. This rag here? It's a goddamn mass killing. I probably shot a hundred loads into it."

"That's disgusting," said Jeremiah.

"Like you don't got a cum rag."

"I don't."

"Then what do you do?"

"I cum in a sock."

Max made a disgusted face. "Then what? You put it on and wear it?"

"Fuck no. I just use it for that."

"For blowin' loads into?"

"Yeah," said Jeremiah, nodding.

"So it's basically the same thing."

Jeremiah shrugged.

Max moved towards Jim Bob, holding the rag in front of his face.

Jim Bob glared at him. *"So help me God, you*

put that rag in my mouth, I'll kill you and every motherfucker you've ever known!"

Max grinned and put it to Jim Bob's mouth. Jim Bob tried to turn his head and clench his mouth closed, but Max forced the rag in. Jim Bob lowered his head, the rag sticking out his mouth. He was crying like a baby.

"What now, Boss?" asked Jeremiah.

"Cocoa wants us to stick ice picks in his eyes."

"I always thought that was kinda fucked up."

"I heard of a guy got an ice pick stuck in his dickhole," said Max. "Jammed in there like a musket."

Jeremiah flinched.

"Who's gonna do it?" asked Jeremiah.

"I don't like it, but Cocoa says I gotta be the one to stick the ice picks in."

Jeremiah slumped a bit. "I was hopin' I could do it."

Max nodded, staring at Jim Bob. "She just said I had to do the ice picks. She didn't say nothin' 'bout the rest."

Jeremiah lit up. "So what you want me to do? I wanna hurt him, but I don't wanna stick the ice pick in his dick hole or any shit like that. I'm not really into messin' with dude's cocks."

"How about this? How 'bout I let you shoot him a couple times?"

Jim Bob grunted. He was looking at them with big eyes, trying to move but unable to due to his restraints.

"I get to shoot the cracker?" Jeremiah asked.

"You can't kill him, but you can shoot him in other places. Arms and legs. Shit like that. But he gotta be alive for the ice picks."

Jeremiah was staring at Jim Bob like a lion eyeing a gazelle. "Cool."

"Better use the silencer," said Max. "We don't want him makin' too much noise. There's neighbors downstairs. Most of 'em are ours, but there's still some civilians here."

Jeremiah frowned. "I ain't got no silencer."

"There's one in the desk drawer."

"Good," said Jeremiah, moving around the desk. "Which drawer?"

"Top."

Jeremiah pulled the drawer open and rifled through it, finally locating the silencer. He fumbled with it, saying, "This don't fit."

Jim Bob was grunting, watching this.

Max looked at Jeremiah. "Shit. I don't have another silencer, but maybe you could just shoot him once. One shot won't bother anybody too much."

"Just one?" asked Jeremiah, disappointed.

"Yeah, so you better make it count."

Jeremiah was standing there, gripping his pistol, looking Jim Bob up and down. "I'm gonna shoot him in his dick."

Jim Bob grunted loud, jerking around.

"You didn't wanna stab his dick, but you'll shoot it?"

"It ain't the same. Shootin' a motherfucker and holdin' his dick to stick an ice pick in it are two different things."

"I guess it's all how you look at it."

Jeremiah raised his pistol and aimed it at Jim Bob's dick.

"You know," said Max, "maybe if you pressed the pistol right up against his dick it would kinda muffle the sound. It would probably hurt worse too."

A big smile spread across Jeremiah's face. "Good thinkin', Boss." He moved towards Jim Bob, leaning down to press the tip of his pistol against his crotch. He looked into Jim Bob's frightened eyes. Jeremiah looked down and saw that Jim Bob had pissed himself.

"You pissed on Cocoa's chair," said Max. "She ain't gonna like that."

Suddenly, the deafening roar of Jeremiah firing the pistol filled the room. It was louder than either of them had expected. “I thought it woulda muffled it, bein' up against his dick like that,” said Max. Jim Bob was moaning loudly, trying to scream.

“Your turn now, Boss,” said Jeremiah.

Max didn't wanna do it, but he had no choice. Reluctantly, he walked over to the desk and picked up one of the two ice picks. He held it for a moment, staring at it. His stomach was starting to knot up. He looked over at Jim Bob, rocking and moaning. Max moved slowly towards him. He held the ice pick up, right in front of Jim Bob's face. The tip was only a few inches from his eye. As Max held it there, trying to muster up the nerve, he felt his stomach roll. Suddenly, he started to vomit, throwing up all over Jim Bob's face and shirt.

“You okay, Boss?” asked Jeremiah.

Max was leaned over, trying to recover. “I'm not sure I can do this,” he said.

“Let me do it. *Please?*”

Max stood up straight, turning towards Jeremiah. He used his sleeve to wipe puke from his lips. “Cocoa says I gotta do it, and I gotta do what she says.”

“Please let me do it,” repeated Jeremiah. “I won't tell nobody.”

“You promise?”

"Cross my fuckin' heart, Boss. I would never do that. I ain't tryin' to fuck up nobody's shit. I ain't tryin' to hurt anybody. I just wanna poke out some eyes."

Max sighed. He handed Jeremiah the ice pick. "Fine," he said. "But this gotta stay between us."

Jeremiah looked at Jim Bob. "It's Christmas-time, motherfucker."

TWENTY-FIVE

CHINO AND ERICKA were in the stolen car, down the street from Cocoa's apartment building. Chino knew Cocoa wouldn't be there, but he might be able to find out where she was.

Jodeci was on the stereo. Chino was watching the two guards standing outside the entrance as he nodded to the music. He turned towards Ericka, looking serious, and she believed he was about to say something important. Instead, he said, "Superman sucks."

"Huh?"

"I was just sitting here thinkin' about it."

"That Superman sucks?"

"Dobbs liked Superman. We used to argue

about it. I always thought Superman was the shittiest, most bullshit superhero ever."

"What's wrong with Superman?"

"Everything. You know why? Because he's perfect. Other than gettin' a handful of Kryptonite, you can't do shit to him. And Kryptonite isn't just layin' around, despite how frequently super-villains seem to find it. Superman is boring as fuck."

"He was the first one though."

"Yeah, but he was terrible. But nobody knew because there weren't any other superheroes to compare him to. But now that we have others, you can see how shitty he is. The dude is trash, Ericka. I don't know why he's still around. His just bein' the first don't make him good. It's like, remember how they used to use leeches as medicine?"

"What the hell, Chino?"

"Bear with me. My point is, just because we used leeches first don't mean we gotta use 'em today when we got better medicine. So, we don't need Superman now that we got better superheroes."

"I think I married a crazy person," said Ericka.

"And how come nobody can see Clark Kent is Superman? He looks like the same fuckin' guy, only without glasses. What the fuck are these? Magic glasses? That shit don't make sense." He sat there staring at the building for a moment. "I dunno. I guess I was just thinkin' 'bout Dobbs."

"You miss him?"

"Almost as much as..." He stopped himself. They both knew where he was going, and Ericka could see the tears in his eyes.

She changed the subject. "How many guys you think there are up there?"

"Maybe fifteen. I dunno. Don't matter though. This ain't my first rodeo. I can handle it."

"*We* can handle it."

"I don't want you up there."

"Try and stop me."

"Really, I don't want you there."

"'Cause I'm a woman?"

"No," he said. "There's a difference between you and me. We ain't the same. You kill people, yeah, but I'm a pro. There's a big difference. These guys here, they're gonna be pros, too."

"What about the two hitters I killed? And what about the guys at Dobbs' funeral?"

"I'll give you the guys in the kitchen," he said. "And Joe Woody's punk ass. But the other guy? Nah. He was a nobody. That shit don't count."

"He was a hitter."

"You don't know that."

"Either way, I'm goin'. If you ever want sex again, I'm goin'."

Chino threw up his hands. "I don't like it."

"You don't have to. Now let's go do this."

Chino sighed. "Let's go."

Chino turned to open the door and Ericka said, "You forgot somethin'."

He turned to her, smiling, and they kissed.

THEY WERE WALKING towards the building. The guards hadn't spotted them yet. It was just as it had been the last time Chino had been here; the guards were distracted, standing around bull-shitting.

"Hang back and watch me," Ericka said.

"No way in hell."

"Bitch please," she said. "Just hang back."

"Fuck no."

"You do it and I'll reward you later."

Chino considered this. "The butt?"

"Maybe. Just stay here until after I talk to the guards."

"I don't like it."

Their eyes locked and she said. "Promise, Chino."

"Okay, I promise. But I don't like it."

"Duly noted." Chino didn't feel good about it, but he hung back, ducking into a doorway. His stomach hurt, and he considered following her, but he'd promised he wouldn't.

Ericka walked towards the guards. The big one, a white dude with a flat-top who looked like a linebacker, saw her first. He started to smile, and it was obvious he didn't know who she was. Now the other guard, a Korean guy, was checking her out. "Hey, mama," he said.

She stopped in front of them. "How you fellas doin'?"

"Better now," said the linebacker.

"Yeah, we good. How 'bout you?" asked the Korean.

"I'm good," she said, laying it on thick. "I'm *real* good."

"I'll bet you are," said the linebacker.

"You lookin' real good in that skirt and them boots," said the Korean.

"Ahhh, that's sweet," she said. "I was wonderin' if you fellas might do me a favor?"

The linebacker grinned. "Anything for a pretty girl like you."

She smiled. "How about I give you both head?"

The two men were startled and confused, which amused Ericka. No woman in the world would be dumb enough to fall for this. It could only work on stupid men with their ever-raging hard-ons.

The linebacker leaned in. "I'm sure we could accommodate you."

"Yeah, I think we could," said the Korean, grinning.

She smiled as she came swooping upward with two butterfly knives, one in each hand. The guys were still smiling when she sliced their throats simultaneously in a single fluid motion. They did the whole dying thing, hands around their throats, blood seeping out between their fingers. Their bodies convulsed, and their eyes were as big as cue balls before they plopped onto the pavement.

Ericka turned towards Chino. She waved for him. When Chino reached her, he said, "Jesus Christ, Ericka. How did you do that?"

"Maybe I'm good like you. You ever thinka that?"

"I always knew you were," he said. "I just didn't know how good."

He leaned in and they kissed, standing over the bodies.

TWENTY-SIX

MAX WAS STANDING in the office with a putter, hitting—and mostly missing—golf balls into a World's Best Boss mug. Each time he missed, Jeremiah would look up from the Mack Bolan book he was reading and smirk.

"You golf, Jerry?" asked Max.

"Nah, Boss. Niggas don't golf."

"How you figure? Look at Tiger Woods."

"What about him?"

"He's black and he plays golf."

"Black people ain't all the same. Tiger Woods playin' golf is like Eminem rappin' or Larry Bird hoopin'. It happens, but it don't happen all that much. Besides, Tiger Woods ain't black."

Max looked at him, confused. "What's that mean?"

"Tiger Woods is about as black as you, Max."

"I don't get it."

"Don't worry about it."

"I had no idea," said Max, putting and missing again. "I always thought Tiger was black. But I dunno. I don't know shit about that."

Jeremiah chuckled. "You right."

"I really thought all your people golfed."

"I suspect there's a few things you think we do that we don't."

"For instance?"

"Love watermelon and chicken."

"You don't like watermelon and chicken?"

"I like chicken, sure, but I probably eat the same amount as you do."

"And watermelon?"

"I don't eat that shit. Watermelon's nasty, all them seeds and shit."

Max shook his head as he lined up his shot. "Watermelon is good." Before he could put again, the phone rang. Max stopped and pulled it out of his pocket, looking at it. It was Cocoa. He looked at Jeremiah and nodded his head towards the door. Jeremiah stood and walked out.

"Hey, Boss, what's up?"

"The sky, motherfucker. Did you do what I asked you?"

"Yes, ma'am."

"With the ice picks?"

"One in each eye."

"You sure you did it right?"

"Are there different ways?"

"There's different ways to do everything."

"What ways are there?"

"There's the right way and there's the wrong way," she said. "And that's usually the way you do things, Maxy."

WHEN CHINO and Ericka strode through the front door, the wooden chair where the interior guard always sat was empty. Chino pointed at it with his pistol. "There's supposed to be a guy there," he said. "Second line of defense. For a long time, it was an old Irish guy named Chuckles."

"Maybe he retired."

"No, I retired him. He was always readin' *Spiderman* comics." He looked at her. "Spidey's a *real* superhero. Not like punk-ass Superman."

"You need to see a shrink, baby," Ericka said.

The bathroom door opened, and a fat man

emerged, zipping up his trousers. He was looking down at first, not seeing them.

"Hey there," said Ericka.

The guy looked up, startled. But he was even more startled by Chino's bullet blasting through his face. He stood there wavering a second, his blood and brains on the wall behind. Then, finally, he toppled over.

Ericka pointed towards a security camera on the ceiling.

"Those are new," said Chino. He winked at her. "I think me killin' all Cocoa's guys is the reason it's there."

"I've known some worthless rat fucks in my time, Maxy, but you take the cake," said Cocoa. "You fuck up so much I'll bet you couldn't fuck up if you were on bottom."

"Cocoa," he said, trying to calm her.

"I've had six *consiglieres*. *Six!* And guess what?"

"I'm the worst?"

"No contest."

"You can't do nothin' right," she said. "Remember when you asked me why I fucked with Chino, the one guy you don't fuck with?"

"I do."

"You were right. I hate to admit it, but you were. For once in your miserable fuckin' existence, you were right. That was a *huge* mistake. But you know what? That wasn't even close to the biggest mistake I've made. Not even close. The biggest mistake I ever made was hirin' you. That makes me question my own sanity. Knowin' what I know now, I wouldn't hire you to clean shit-covered toilets."

THE ELEVATOR STOPPED on the fourth floor. When the doors slid open, there were three guys with guns waiting. Chino started firing through the crack as the doors started to separate. He'd shot two of them already—both in the head—when he realized Ericka had thrown a knife into the throat of the third.

He looked at her. "You're pretty handy with that."

She went to the body and pulled the knife from the man's throat. She turned and looked at Chino. "I've got a lot of talents."

"Who you tellin'?"

Ericka got back on the elevator, and Chino pressed the button.

. . .

"I WOULD FIRE YOU, Max, but you're gonna be dead soon anyway," said Cocoa.

"You think so?"

"I *know* so."

"You sound optimistic."

"I ain't optimistic at all," she said. "'Cause if Chino gets you, he gets one step closer to me. I don't give a fuck if you die, but me, that's a different thing. 'Cause I don't wanna die, Maxy."

"Good for you."

"It's the truth, Maxy," she said. "You shoulda heard more of it. Your parents shoulda told you how worthless you were. They should've aborted your ass. You know what? Now that I think about it, I oughta track them motherfuckers down and kill 'em for not doin' it. You know that? Some people are put here to do great things, Maxy."

"But not me."

"No, not you. *Me*. I'm talkin' 'bout me. But then there's people put here to do nothin'. Then there's a third group. That's your group."

"Whaddaya mean?"

"That group exists just to fuck things up for everybody else. I believe in God, Maxy, and I think maybe you're my punishment for all the bad shit I've done. I really do. You're a goddamn piece of shit fuck up. And Chino's gonna show up, Maxy. And when he does, you're gonna die a slow, painful death. And when Chino does show up, you better keep your mouth shut. You don't say a word about me, Maxy. Not one."

"I would never do that."

"Listen," she said, suddenly calm. "I'm gonna call in the cavalry on this. We're down to a skeleton crew. Chino done killed all our top guys. You got a few guys there, I got a few guys here. Good guys, but not good enough. Not when it comes to this motherfucker Chino."

"So what?"

"I got a plan. I'm gonna call for backup. I'm gonna bring Saint Lewis in. He's the only guy who's anywhere close to Chino's level."

"What if he's tied up?"

"Money talks, and I got money. Enough money to untie his ass. I figure I'll get him and a couple other big guns to come in from outta town and fix this. I'll keep Saint Lewis here with me to watch the farmhouse and then send the other two after Chino and that bitch."

"You think she's with him?"

"Hard to say," said Cocoa. "If he's smart, he done stashed her ass away somewhere. But either way, we'll find her."

"Saint Lewis, huh?" asked Max. "They say he's good."

"He is, Maxy. But you ain't never seen Chino do his thing. Those two, they're cut from the same cloth. Both of 'em are natural born killers if there ever was such a thing. You want a motherfucker dead, you call them."

"If Saint Lewis is so good, why ain't he workin' for us now?"

"I wish he was," said Cocoa. "He's been workin' for Frankie DeSantis. I convince Frankie to send Saint Lewis up for this, I'm gonna owe Frankie big time. Probably a major piece of my action."

"Is it worth it?"

"What do you think, Maxy? It's the difference between bein' alive and bein' dead. So yeah, it's worth it. And if we can get those guys down here ASAP, they just might save us both."

"Then we'll be square, you and me?" asked Max.

"I didn't say that. But you play your cards right, maybe I'll just demote you."

"You'll demote me?"

"Would you rather be dead?"

Max paused. "Okay, demote me. I don't wanna die. I'm sorry I caused you problems."

"You can't help it, Maxy," she said. "It's who you are."

The door opened and Jeremiah poked his

head in. There was a strange look on his face. Max waved him to go away, but Jeremiah just stood there.

"Hold on a sec," Max told Cocoa. He looked at the bodyguard. "I'm on the phone, Jerry."

Jeremiah took another step forward, and Max could see Chino behind him with his pistol to the back of his head. Then he saw Ericka behind Chino.

"They're here," Max told Cocoa.

"Who?"

"Chino and the girl."

"Damn," said Cocoa. "This'll be our last conversation then. Whatever you do, just keep your fuckin' mouth shut. Don't say nothin'. You're gonna die, but you can at least die with dignity."

Max hung up.

Chino looked at Max and winked. Chino squeezed the trigger, shooting Jeremiah in the back of the head, blowing his brains out through his eye socket.

"You blew out his fuckin' eye!" said Max.

Chino grinned. "You ever seen a black guy with blue eyes before? Cause his eye was blew —*blew the fuck out.*"

Max stared at him with his mouth open.

"Terrible joke," said Ericka.

"Yeah, yeah," said Chino.

"I got guards!" screamed Max. *"They'll get you!"*

Max's eyes turned to the wall of surveillance screens now, seeing nothing but dead bodies lying all over in various hallways.

"They're all dead," said Ericka.

"You're last of the Mohicans," said Chino.

Max was standing there staring at them when he realized he had a putter in his hand. He started to raise it, but Chino said, "You don't wanna do that, pal. I got a gun on you. I can put a slug through your face before you can get that thing raised."

Max dropped the putter.

Ericka motioned towards his chair. "Have a seat."

Max looked at the chair, staring at it like it was something foreign he'd never seen before. He was dazed and confused, moving slowly. He sat.

Ericka moved towards him, picking up the putter.

Max knew this wouldn't be good.

"You wanna play some golf?" she asked.

"No," said Max. "I'll tell you everything." He looked at Chino. "Maybe we can make a deal. I tell you what I know, you let me live."

"No deal," said Ericka. Max stared at her, his mouth open. He looked over at Chino.

"You heard her," said Chino.

Max slumped in his chair. "If I tell you, would you at least let me die a fast death?" He looked at Ericka again. "And keep her from bashing my head in with the putter?"

Ericka looked at Chino, and Chino could see she wanted to hit him. He shrugged. "She's an independent woman. But I'll see what I can do."

Max looked at Chino desperately. "Maybe I don't make a deal then. What if I don't tell you?"

Chino and Ericka chuckled.

"That's not an option," said Chino. "You gonna tell us what we wanna know. The only difference is how bad I hurt you to get the information, and how much I make you suffer after. You tell me now, it'll be quick."

"Fair enough," said Max, sounding deflated. "Cocoa is staying in a farmhouse near Dryden."

"Where's Dryden? I never heard of that."

"It's way upstate."

"Where's the house?"

"I don't know," said Max.

"She didn't tell you?"

"No. I swear she didn't. She said she didn't want me to know in case..." He looked up at Chino.

"In case I got to you."

Max nodded.

"You know what color the house is?"

"I don't."

Chino shifted from one foot to the other, his pistol still on Max, trying to decide what else to ask. Finally, he said, "How many guys she got with her?"

"Seven, I think," said Max, feeling slightly pleased he hadn't told Chino about Saint Lewis. At least he'd kept that to himself.

"That's all you know?" asked Chino.

"That's it," said Max.

Max was staring at Chino when the putter struck him in the side of the head.

TWENTY-SEVEN

Cocoa was on the couch, stroking her poodle. There was some lovey-dovey shit with Sandra Bullock on the television, and Cocoa was staring out the window. She saw two cats humping in the yard, one looking like it was raping the other, but she paid them no mind. Her thoughts were on Chino. She knew it was her fault—she could have just let him go—but she was still angry with him. For a number of reasons. First, she was angry at him for falling in love with the bitch. Second, she was angry at him for killing so many of her guys. Third, she was angry he was coming to kill her.

She didn't want to call Mikey Constantino, but she saw no other way. She sat there, staring at her phone. She picked it up and punched in the number. The phone rang four times and Cocoa thought she was gonna get voicemail. But she didn't.

"Hello, Cocoa," said Mikey.

"I need your help."

Mikey was an older guy—an intermediate who worked with all the organizations. When someone needed help from one organization or had beef with another, they called Mikey. Mikey then arranged things or stepped in to arbitrate. This was the way it had always been done. Cocoa had never asked for help from any of the other organizations, and she hated having to do it now.

"I got a problem," she said.

"Chino Genetti," he said. "Everybody knows your situation."

This embarrassed her, which pissed her off. She'd scrapped her way up from a hard neighborhood to the top of the food chain, and she hated being seen as weak.

"How can I help?" Mikey asked.

"I wanna reach out to Frankie."

"You want Saint Lewis."

"Yeah."

"It's gonna cost you."

"What do you want?"

"It ain't what I want," said Mikey. "I'll get my share, but Frankie is gonna want a pretty penny for lending him to you. Especially in an emergency situation like this."

"Emergency situation?"

"Let's not fuck around, Cocoa. You ain't never called nobody for help, ever. And this is Chino we're talkin' about. We all know what that guy can do. Nobody knows more than you, so let's cut the shit. If you're callin' me, you're in dire need. And let's face it, Saint Lewis is the only hitter who's better than Chino."

"You think he's better?" she asked.

"You'd better hope he is."

"I need Saint Lewis and two other A-listers."

"Three hitters?"

"Three."

"Fuckin' Chino's got you scared."

Cocoa said nothing.

"Let me see what I can do."

"Thanks, Mikey."

"I'll call Frankie and get back with you."

Mikey hung up and Cocoa sighed.

She was overcome with a surge of anger and frustration. In a flash of rage, she grabbed the poodle around its midsection, hurling it across the room. It yelped in pain as it crashed into the television.

Cocoa looked at the damage she'd done. *"Goddamn you, Chino."*

Frankie was sitting on his eight-year-old daughter Vanessa's bed, reading *Goodnight Moon* to Vanessa and her twin sister Carmen. He stopped reading and looked at the girls. *"Goodnight kittens?"* he said. *"Goodnight mittens?* This book is bullshit."

"I like it, Daddy," said Carmen.

"Me too," said Vanessa.

"You sure you don't want me to read you somethin' else?"

"No, Daddy," said Vanessa.

"Please read it," said Carmen.

"Okay, sure," said Frankie, looking at the book again. Just then, his phone started to ring. He looked at it, seeing it was a New Jersey number. He looked at the girls. "I should take this," he said. "Gimme a minute." He answered the phone. "Who the fuck is this?"

"Heya Frank, it's Mikey."

"Mikey G or Mikey C?"

"Mikey C."

"Good, good. I'm gonna kill that cocksucker Mikey G."

"I just got a call from Cocoa."

"Yeah?" asked Frankie. "What's that cunt want?"

"She wants your help."

"With the Chino thing?"

"Yeah."

"Why'd she fuck with him in the first place?"

"I think it was a pride thing."

"It was a stupid thing is what it was. So, what's she want?"

"Saint Lewis."

"Of course she does. Everybody wants Saint Lewis."

"Nobody's better," said Mikey.

"What's she prepared to give?"

"She didn't say, but I'd venture she'd give just about anything. After all, he's the only thing between her and a ticket to hell."

"What would you ask for, it was you?"

"It ain't my place."

"But I'm askin'."

"It was me," said Mikey, "I'd ask for ten percent of everything."

"That's fair." He thought about it. "Tell that cunt bitch I want twenty."

"Twenty?"

"It's a seller's market. She's got no choice."

"I guess not."

"I run the risk of Saint Lewis gettin' killed.

He gets killed, then what I got? Bupkis. So you call her black ass back and tell her she can use Saint Lewis for twenty percent. Nothin' less. She don't like it, she can go to the store and buy another Saint Lewis. I got news for ya, there ain't no more. The stores are sold out. There's just two in that league—Saint Lewis and Chino fuckin' Genetti."

"Alright, I'll tell her," said Mikey.

Frankie clicked off the phone. The little girls looked at him.

"What's a cunt bitch?" asked Vanessa.

Frankie grinned. "You know your grandma Marie?"

"Yes," both girls answered.

"She's a real ball-breaker," said Frankie.

"Is she a cunt bitch?" asked Carmen.

"A big fat one."

Cocoa was drinking a glass of vodka, staring at the broken television. She already missed Dee Dee, whom the boys had put down due to a broken leg. She'd always known she wasn't really a pet person as she'd killed every pet she'd ever owned, but still had hope that maybe one day she could do it. While she was considering this, her phone rang. It was Mikey.

She answered. "What did you find out?"

"I spoke to Frankie."

"Yeah?"

"He'll give you Saint Lewis."

"How much?"

"Twenty."

"Twenty?!" she screamed. *"Are you outta your rabbit-ass mind?"*

"Cocoa."

"You call that maricon motherfucker and you tell him he can go fuck himself sideways with a paring knife!"

Mikey started to speak, but Cocoa hurled the phone across the room, watching it crash into the wall by the busted television. She sat there staring at it for a moment and then realized what she'd done. She rushed towards the phone, snatching it up to see if it was alright. The screen was cracked like a spiderweb. She pushed the button and called Mikey back.

"Yeah?" asked Mikey, sounding annoyed.

"Tell Frankie I'll do it."

"You still want the other two hitters?"

"Please."

TWENTY-EIGHT

Joe the Rabbi was crouched, leaning over the the tub, sawing the dead guy's leg off. Cutting through the thigh was always tough. This was the part of his job Joe hated most. Worst thing was, this guy he was cutting wasn't even for work. Just some Irish prick he'd met at the bar. The guy had had a few too many drinks and had started mouthing off about the screwdriver Joe was drinking. "Only fags drink fruity drinks," the guy had said, laughing. Well, fuck him. The prick wasn't laughing now. He was nearly finished sawing through the thigh when the cellphone sitting on the toilet rang. Joe looked over at it.

"Jesus Harold Christ," he muttered, dropping the saw. He reached for the phone with his blood-covered hand. He answered.

"I'm kinda busy here, Mikey," he said.

"I'll keep it short. I got a job for you."

"I got jobs up to my fuckin' eyeballs."

"Philly keepin' you that busy?"

"You know," said Joe, "City of brotherly love."

Mikey chuckled. "This one pays well."

"How well?"

"More than you'll get killin' your next twelve guys in Philly."

"Okay," said Joe, nodding. "Where's is it?"

"New York City."

"Jesus fuck. I hate New York."

"But you like gettin' paid."

Joe nodded. "This is true. What's the job?"

"It's a job for Cocoa."

"Why can't her guys do it?"

"'Cause they're all dead."

"Yeah?" asked Joe. "Who killed 'em?"

"Your target."

"Anybody I know?"

"Chino Genetti."

"Holy shit," said Joe. "I'll do it."

"You're not intimidated?"

"Don't nobody intimidate me. Maybe they should, but they don't. And I'm bored here. I can use the challenge. Besides, I get to meet Chino Genetti and maybe even kill 'im. That would be one hell of a notch on my belt."

"You a cowboy now?"

"I always been a cowboy."

"So you're in?"

"Fuckin' A."

HER NAME WAS CHARLIE DANIELS, like the country singer, but she didn't sing. Most guys who crossed her path and lived—many had busted noses—said she was the toughest bitch they'd ever met. Men found her sexy in a tough bitch sorta way with her cropped blonde hair and her strong jawline. But she wasn't no beauty queen. No, Charlie was as tough a human as God had ever made. And she was as lean and muscular as a panther but twice as dangerous. This fucker Benji was finding out the hard way.

He was dancing around like the newbie he was, thinking he could take her because she was a girl. He was dancing around like he was the reincarnation of Muhammad Ali. But the little punk wasn't Muhammad Ali. He was just a sorry motherfucker who thought it might be fun to take up boxing. Maybe get in shape while he was at it. In about ten seconds, he was gonna be an unconscious motherfucker who would later wake up and rethink his choices.

But for now, they were in the ring. They were just sparring, but the fight was intense. When Charlie had suggested they box without head gear, Benji had jumped at the chance. Probably a woman-beater, thought Charlie. Maybe, maybe not, but she was about to make him pay like he was.

She moved in on him now, moving to her left, faking him out, then coming in with a hard right, catching him in his temple. The punch connected solidly and for a moment it looked like a scene from *Raging Bull* with Benji's eyes rolling back, his head rocking to his left, and sweat flying off in slow motion. But that moment passed quickly, and Benji was unconscious on the mat.

"He got his ass knocked out," said one of the boxers watching.

Charlie started taking off her gloves. As she did, she looked up at Terry, the old trainer who owned the gym. He was shaking his head. "Come on, Charlie," he said. "Why'd you hafta go and do that? It was the kid's first time."

She took her mouth guard out. "If he's smart, it'll be his last."

Terry shook his head. "You're a tough kid,"

he said. The other boxers whooped and make jokes about Benji getting knocked out. But nobody was making fun of Charlie. Christ no. Charlie had knocked most of them out half a dozen times. Those she'd only knocked out once or twice were the guys too scared to fight her again.

She climbed down out the ring and headed for the locker room.

"That all for you?" asked one of the guys.

"Kickin' Benji's ass wore me out," she said.

She made her way to the same locker she'd used for the past seven years. She opened it and grabbed a towel, using it to dry her face. She then reached in for her phone and earbuds, thinking she might run and listen to music. When she looked at the phone, she saw she'd missed a call from Mikey Constantino.

Hopefully a job, she thought. She'd pissed away her money fucking around and drinking, and she had bills to pay. She called Mikey.

"Hey Mikey," she said. "It's Charlie."

"Hey Charlie. I got a job for you."

"Good. I need one."

"It pays well," he said.

"Sounds good."

"Don't you wanna know anything about it?"

"All I need to know is where I go."

"This guy is different," said Mikey. "He's pretty tough."

"I'm tough too," she said. "And a job's a job. Ain't nobody different, Mikey. They all bleed, and they all die. I'll kill anyone. Just pay me my money and we're straight. Where's the job?"

"The big apple."

Charlie nodded. "I can dig it. When do I leave?"

"As soon as possible."

TWENTY-NINE

Ericka woke up in the El Rancho Motor Inn around seven. Chino was sitting up in bed, wearing only his checkered boxers and watching ESPN. She looked at him, blinking herself awake. "Why you watchin' ESPN? You don't watch sports."

Chino shrugged. "I miss the days when I actually cared."

"What made you stop caring?"

"I used to watch basketball with Dobbs. When he moved, all my interest went with him."

"You missin' Dobbs?"

"I'll always miss him." He turned back towards the TV. "He was the only friend I had."

"What about me?"

"You know what I mean. It's different."

"How's that?"

He grinned. "I never fucked Dobbs."

"You haven't fucked me lately either."

"You gotta be kiddin'. We had sex in the stolen car just yesterday."

She lay there for a few minutes before asking, "What time is it?"

"Probably about seven, seven-thirty."

"What time did you wake up?"

"About three."

"Three?"

"I couldn't sleep. Switched on the TV and there was an old Bogart movie on. *Treasure of the Sierra Madre.* You ever seen it?"

"No. What's it about?"

"It's about some guys in the middle of nowhere mining for gold."

"It sounds riveting," she said sarcastically.

"It don't matter what it sounds like, it's good."

"Chino?"

"Yeah?"

"Do you love me?"

"You know I do."

"How much?"

"More than there's kids say Michael Jackson fucked 'em."

"That's a bunch."

"That's how much I love you."

"Can I ask you somethin'?" she asked.

"Anything."

"I'm cravin' a breakfast burrito."

"So?"

"Do you love me enough to go get me one?"

"I don't even know where they sell 'em here."

"If you loved me, you'd go find one."

He nodded, looking at the TV again. "I go do this, you're gonna owe me."

"Yeah?"

He turned towards her, grinning. "You bet your ass."

"Get the burrito and we'll talk."

Ericka was brushing her teeth when she heard the knock. *Dammit Chino*, she thought. He must have forgotten the key card. She leaned forward and spit a glob of toothpaste into the sink.

There was a second knock.

"Hold on a sec," she said.

Wearing only her pink underwear and black bra, she went to the door and opened it. It wasn't Chino. It was a heavyset Italian with a goatee.

"I'm the fuckin' maid," he said. Before Ericka realized what was happening, the guy socked her in the eye, sending her reeling back onto the floor. She looked up at him as he stepped in, closing the door.

"You must be the bitch," he said.

"And you must be the dumbfuck."

He grinned.

She stared up at him. "Can I tell you somethin'?"

"What?"

"That goatee you got..."

"You like it?"

"Ain't nobody worth a fuck had a goatee since Bill Clinton was fuckin' fat secretaries." She looked at him. "But you ain't worth a fuck."

He stood there grinning. "You don't know shit about me."

"I know you got an IQ that's even smaller than your dick."

"You're a mouthy bitch." He looked towards the bathroom. "Chino in there?"

"No," she said. "He ain't here."

"Where's he at?"

"Probably fuckin' your mom."

"That ain't nice," he said, frowning. "I'm gonna ask you again: where's Chino?"

"And I'm gonna tell you again—fuckin' your mom."

The guy stood there grinning. He rolled his

head around on his neck, his head upwards, and then stared down at her menacingly. "That so, cunt?" He moved towards her, kicking her hard with his steel-toed boot. It hurt like a mother-fucker, sharp pain shooting through her side. "You want more of that, bitch? There's a lot more where that came from. Now, we gonna do this the easy way, or the hard way?"

"Which was that?"

"That was the easy way. It gets a lot harder from here. Now, where's Chino?"

Ericka nodded. "Okay. He went to find Cocoa. He went to kill her."

He seemed unaffected by this. "And he left a pretty little thing like you here, all by your lonesome?"

"I can take care of myself."

The guy sat his .45 on the nightstand. Looking down at her with a creepy look in his eyes, he said, "I'm gonna teach you a lesson, bitch." He reached down and started unzipping his trousers. "Mouthy bitches tend to be less mouthy when they got somethin' in their mouths."

Ericka knew she was in trouble. If she was gonna act, now was the time. Seeing nothing else within reaching distance, she grabbed the handle of the dresser drawer and yanked it open, hoping to find a bible or something—*anything*—she could hurl at him. She sat up, peering into the drawer, but found nothing. In that instant, he was on her, his pants halfway down. He was still in his tighty-whities. He smelled like cheap dollar store cologne. He straddled her, grabbing her arms and holding her down. "You smell real good," he said.

She had a flashback of Mr. Tanner forcing himself on her. She could smell Mr. Tanner's cologne—a better brand, but still too strong—in her nostrils, and she was transported back to that moment. The moment in her life when she'd felt the most helpless. She tried to knee goatee guy in the balls but was unable to raise her leg as he had it pinned down. He was right up in her face, hot garlic breath in her nose, overpowering the smell of his cologne, and he was staring into her eyes. He licked his lips.

She spit in his face. He grinned.

"Fiesty bitch, huh? That's the way I like 'em. It ain't fun if the bitch don't put up a fight."

"Fuck you," she growled, still struggling to break free.

He leaned forward, moving his mouth around to the side of her face, kissing her. She growled a guttural sound as she tried to fend him off. As they wrestled, the man kissing her neck, she was unable to hear Chino enter the room. She wasn't aware he was there until he grabbed the guy, pulling him off. Goatee guy grunted, not sure what was happening. Before he regained his bearings, Chino was punching him. *Hard.* The guy fell over Ericka, and Chino was punching his face, again and again. Ericka could see the guy's face changing shape, losing definition as his jaw shattered. Ericka pulled herself back away from the guy, and she saw Chino punch his nose so hard it made a crunching sound, bending sideways.

When Joe the Rabbi woke up, he found himself lying in the tub with the barrel of his own gun in his mouth. His eyes wide, he stared at Ericka. She had her finger on the trigger and was smiling a wide "I-just-won-the-fuckin'-lottery" smile.

"Say goodnight, Gracie," she said.

With the .45 in his mouth, Joe couldn't say shit.

"We should ask him where Cocoa is," Chino said.

As Ericka stared into Joe's eyes, Joe could see her excitement.

"We need to find Cocoa," Chino insisted.

Ericka squeezed the trigger, the sound of the

gun magnified by the tub, and Joe's blood and brains were everywhere.

"Jesus, Ericka. Why'd you do that?"

"Motherfucker pissed me off."

"Remind me never to piss you off."

She grinned. "Shut up and kiss me."

THIRTY

Cocoa was sitting in the porch swing, staring at the sky, thinking about Chino. It had been a mistake going after him. She saw that now. She should have left well enough alone. But leaving shit alone had never been her strong suit. And now she was paying for it. As she thought about this, she heard the sound of an engine. She turned and saw an old farmer in an old orange pickup coming down the gravel road. Cocoa watched him with curiosity, becoming even more curious when he pulled into the driveway. He parked behind one of the three black Escalades.

One of Cocoa's guys, Dane, a big white guy who always wore sunglasses, even inside, looked at her for instruction. She raised her hand, telling him to allow the old man to approach. The old potbellied farmer with a long, gray hillbilly beard got out of the truck. He was wearing a plaid shirt and overalls. Standing beside the truck, he took off his cap, and wiped sweat from his brow with his forearm. He looked at Cocoa on the porch. The old man stood there studying Cocoa and Dane for a moment, and then made his way towards the house. He was about ten feet away when he said, "Howdy, ma'am."

She looked at him. "There somethin' I can do for you?"

"This house has been vacant for a coupla years and now all of a sudden there's all these black SUVs parked here. And you people. You look outta place." He gave her a strange look. "And you. You're..."

She smiled. "I'm *what*?"

"You know."

"Black?"

The old man nodded. "I don't know what the proper terminology is. Colored, I guess. We don't get many of your kind out here, so I figured I'd stop by and see what you were up to."

She smiled. "You wanted to see if we were on the up-and-up? If we were supposed to be here? Or maybe you thought we were just up to no good."

The old man stood there, his hands on his hips, giving her a stern look. "Your guy with the sunglasses here, he's packin' a Glock. So yeah, it looks like you're up to some shit."

"What do you care if Dane's got a gun?"

"New York's not an open carry state. This ain't Texas, you know."

"But you didn't know he had a gun 'til you got here. You came up here 'cause I'm black."

The man nodded. He looked at the SUVs. "But also these." Then he looked at her again, the two of them making eye contact. "But yeah, since you said it, mostly 'cause you're black."

Dane turned and looked at her again. This time Cocoa nodded. Dane stepped off the porch, moving towards the farmer.

The old man put his hands up, stepping back. "I didn't mean nothin'."

Dane grabbed him.

"You caught me on the wrong day, Farmer Joe," said Cocoa. "We're ain't buyin' what you're sellin'."

Dane held him in place. Dane's Glock was in his other hand.

"What's that supposed to mean?" asked the old man.

"Dane," Cocoa said. "You wanna show him what it means?"

Dane looked at her for a moment. "You want me to shoot him?"

"Well, I don't want you to make gingerbread cookies with him."

Dane turned to look at the farmer, raising his Glock as he did.

"Hey, I'm sorry," said the old man. "I didn't mean..."

"You did," said Cocoa. "You thought I was a black bitch, didn't you? And you thought, I'll go down there and bother that black bitch, right?"

"No, no," said the old man. "It's not like that..."

"Guess what, old man? This black bitch don't feel like playin' bullshit peckerwood games today."

"I'm sorry," said the old man, trying to pull away. Dane still had a firm grasp of his arm. He pressed the tip of the Glock against the old man's forehead.

"Dane, drop him."

Dane looked at the old man. Without skipping a beat, he fired the pistol and the farmer crumpled to the ground. Dane stood over him, looking down. "You want me to shoot him again?"

"No," she said. "We better conserve ammo. If Chino shows up, we're gonna need every bullet we got. I want you to take this old bastard around back and get rid of him."

"Bury him?"

"I don't care," said Cocoa. "Bury him, burn him, sink him in the fuckin' pond, whatever. I don't give a flyin' fuck as long as I don't see him again." She looked at the pickup. "Go get Alfonso and have him move the truck. Tell him to put it out in the barn, outta sight. We don't need more nosy neighbors sniffin' 'round. They keep comin' and we keep shootin', we're liable to run outta ammo before Chino shows up. Either that or you'll be too tired from shootin' farmers to stop him."

THE OLD MAN and his pickup were no longer on Cocoa's mind. They were in the bottom of the pond. What was on her mind was Chino and the bitch. If they showed up, she would be dead. They all would.

She stared at the field across the road, thinking. She raised her cracked phone and pushed a button, holding it up to her ear. It rang twice.

"Hello?" said Dennis.

"This your mother," Cocoa said.

Long pause. "I don't have a mother.".

"Look," she said, "I know you're mad and

you don't wanna have anything to do with me. I'm fine with that. But there's some shit goin' down now and there's a good chance I won't be around much longer."

"What does that mean?"

"Chances are good I'm gonna be dead soon."

There was another pause, and Dennis spoke: "Like I said, I don't have a mother." And he hung up, stealing a move from Cocoa's playbook.

"Well, hell," she muttered. She lowered the phone and sat there staring at it. All this was her fault—*all of it*—from the shit with Chino to the situation with her son. She could have just let Chino and the singer go about their business. She could have spared her son's boyfriend's life after she'd learned he was gay. But she hadn't. So what? Life was too short to sit around and dwell on past mistakes. Some decisions were good, some decisions were bad. Fuck it.

She exhaled, staring at the field again. Maybe, just maybe, Saint Lewis would arrive like a knight in shining armor and save her from her mistakes. But honestly, Cocoa wasn't convinced. When Chino had worked for her, she'd bragged to everyone about his being the best in the game, and she believed that. She'd seen the damage he could do time and time again. At best, she figured her odds of survival were 50/50.

Sitting there, she looked to the sky for help. She spoke to the God she hadn't spoken to since she was a child. She searched for the words to a prayer but couldn't remember one. So she winged it. "Dear God in Heaven," she said. "I know I've done a lot of fucked up shit. Really heinous shit. You and me, we both know the things. I don't need to list 'em all. I don't even think I *could* even if I wanted to. So I don't expect you to forgive me. If you're anything like me, you don't forgive nobody for nothin'. But, my grandma used to say you did. So maybe that shit's true. If it is, I'm askin' you to please forgive all the wicked shit I've done." She paused, looking to make sure none of her men were around.

She looked up again. "Please, God, if you're up there, I need your help. I need you to save me." She sat quietly, staring at the sky. Finally, she said, "I need a sign if you're up there, God."

About a minute passed before she heard the black Hummer come rambling down the road, kicking up dust. It slowed in front of the house. Was this Chino? She squinted but couldn't see through the dust. The two guards who were outside with her, Mel and Dane, had their guns up and ready.

The Hummer's door opened and a mountain-sized man climbed out. It wasn't Chino. It was a white guy wearing a gray sports coat. He was roughly twice the size of a fullback, and he was pure muscle. He was bald with muscles bulging out of his neck. It looked like there were muscles bulging out of other muscles. He was the kind of guy who made you think "steroids" the moment you saw him. Despite the guards standing there with their pistols raised, he strode towards them nonchalantly. When Cocoa saw the dragon tattoo on the side of his skull, she knew who he was.

"Fellas," said Cocoa. Both guards remained where they were, their pistols locked on him. "Put your guns down," she said. "This is Saint Lewis."

The two guards looked at one another, kind of shrugged, and lowered their weapons. Saint Lewis strode past them without acknowledging them. He carried himself in a superior manner. And in this world, he *was* superior. He was royalty. He arrived at the steps, his eyes locked with Cocoa's. He stepped up.

"You must be Cocoa," he said.

"I am."

"Everybody calls me Saint."

"Your reputation precedes you," she said. "Everybody knows you."

He smiled. "That's kind of you. And everyone knows about Cocoa, the woman who don't take no shit."

"That'll be on my headstone," she said. "It'll be the thing that kills me."

He took her hand in his, leaned down, and kissed it. "Not if I got anything to say about it," he said. "You're safe."

"You think?"

"I *know*. Chino shows up, he's gonna be a dead motherfucker."

"You're confident."

"No," he said. "Just aware of my talents."

"Chino's good."

He smiled. "But I'm better."

"Have you met Chino?"

"No. But I look forward to killing him."

THIRTY-ONE

Chino and Ericka were in Joe the Rabbi's F-10, driving around Dryden, looking for clues. "You're a Customer" was on the stereo, but neither was listening. They had the windows down, letting the cool air blow in.

"How we gonna find 'em?" asked Ericka. "They could be anywhere. Especially since Max said they're in the country. This whole area is country. It's like a needle in a haystack."

"This haystack ain't that big though."

"So what do we do?"

"I'll ask around, see if anybody has seen a bunch of gangster-lookin' motherfuckers. They ought to stick out like a sore thumb."

Chino pulled into a gas station. He went inside. There was an old Eagles song playing from a radio behind the counter. There was only one customer, an older woman buying scratch-off tickets. Chino milled around until she finished and left. He approached the young guy behind the counter.

"Hey buddy," he said. "I was hopin' maybe you could help me out."

The guy squinted, his head slightly cocked. "What you need?"

"I'm lookin' for somebody."

"Yeah?"

"Have you seen anybody this week who looks out of place?"

The man nodded. "Just one guy."

"What can you tell me about him?"

The guy grinned. "He's you."

"Okay, let's try this." Chino reached into his pocket and pulled out his wallet. He produced a fifty. "This ring any bells?"

The guy's face lit up. "Could be."

"You're not sure?"

"It *almost* makes me remember."

"Almost?"

"Fifty is almost, a hundred is definite."

"You'd definitely remember somethin' for a hundred?"

The guy nodded.

Chino hated being suckered. He pulled out another fifty. "This improve your memory?"

"There was a big guy in here about an hour ago. Muscular bald guy, with a big gaudy dragon tattoo. He was packin'. His gun was under his jacket, but it was obvious. And he was drivin' a big macho-assed black Hummer. The kinda truck guys drive to make up for havin' tiny dicks."

Chino bit his lip. "He had a dragon tattoo?"

"Yeah. Red and green."

"Where was it?"

The guy pointed at the side of his head. "Here."

Chino had heard stories about a hitter with a dragon tattoo on the side of his head. A guy from Chicago who was supposed to be as good as he was. They called him Saint Lewis. Chino didn't know if he was still working, but he was pretty sure it was him.

"You said he was big. How big was he?"

"He looked like the Incredible Hulk if the Hulk used steroids."

"That big, huh?"

"Pretty big."

"He say anything?"

"He asked for directions."

Holy shit, Chino thought. When the guy

saw Chino's expression, he doubled down. "That's gonna cost more."

"What if it isn't the right guy?"

"What if it is?"

Chino nodded, reaching into his wallet and producing a Benny to go with the two fifties. "This is all you get. No more."

The guy shrugged. "Fair enough."

"Where was he goin'?"

"He was lookin' for a farmhouse."

"Where was it?"

"Out on 2000 Road."

"How far's that?"

"Ten miles, give or take."

"Yeah?"

"I can give you the same directions I gave him."

"But it'll cost me?"

The guy shrugged.

"$200 is all you get. If you don't give me those directions, I'm takin' back the money I already gave you." He paused. "And I'm knockin' out your teeth."

The guy shrugged. "You can't blame a guy for tryin'." He turned around, grabbed a piece of paper, and started hunting for a pen. Once he found one, he started scribbling. As he did,

Chino asked, "You see anybody else weird around here lately?"

"Define weird."

"Black Escalades. Could be a few of 'em."

The guy handed him the paper.

"They all go this direction," he said. "There's different ones stop in here every day or so, all of 'em tough-lookin' fuckers. All of 'em look like they're packin'. Look like extras from a crime movie. And one guy, I seen him twice, always has sunglasses on, even when he's inside."

"I hate guys like that."

"Yeah, me too. The only ones who are worse are the ones who wear 'em on the back of their heads."

The guy nodded in agreement. Chino handed him the cash and the guy smiled, saying, "Nice doin' business with you."

Any other day, Chino would have smacked the shit out of him or at least called his mother a whore. But not today. Today he was just happy to have the address. On his way out, Chino grabbed a Snickers bar and held it up. "I'm takin' this," he said. "You don't like it, you can take it out the $200 I gave you."

When Chino got back in the pickup, he said, "I found our needle."

"Already?"

"What can I say? I'm good."

Ericka grinned and kissed him.

"I love you, baby," she said.

"I love you, too."

They drove off, EPMD playing again. They were a couple miles outside of town when Ericka opened her backpack and pulled out the two ice picks. "I can't wait to show Cocoa what I bought her," she said. "Seein' how she loves people gettin' ice picks stuck in their eyes."

Chino didn't take his eyes off the road. "I swear, you two are peas in a pod," he said. "Beautiful women with ice cold hearts." He meant it as a compliment, but all Ericka heard was the part about Cocoa being beautiful. She looked at Chino, blinking. "Hold up. You think that bitch is *beautiful*?"

Chino looked at her, unsure what to say.

"Don't forget I've got ice picks," she said.

"She's pretty, but not as pretty as you."

She glared at him. "You'd better say that."

Chino stared at the road, wondering how he still managed to step on these landmines after all these years. He could feel her stare. "Did you ever *do* anything with her?"

"With who?" he asked, playing dumb.

"You did, didn't you?!"

Chino didn't know what to say, so he said nothing.

"Goddammit, Chino," she said. *"I can't believe you.* Is that why she wants us dead? 'Cause she's in love with you?"

Chino turned and looked at her. "That's not a thing," he said. "We slept together *once.*" Before he could continue, he heard Ericka groan. "It was before you and I knew each other. It didn't mean anything. I promise."

He looked back at the road to avoid oncoming traffic.

"Cocoa wants us dead because she's evil," he said. "It's got nothin' to do with love or jealousy or any of that. It was never like that. She's after us because she doesn't like bein' defied, and I defied her by not killin' you. It's as simple as that. So if you're mad about it, I suggest you take it up with Cocoa."

"Oh, I will," said Ericka. "I'ma take it out *on* her." She was about to say more but was interrupted when another vehicle slammed hard into the back of the pickup, causing them to lurch forward. Chino and Ericka had been distracted, neither realizing there was a Camaro speeding up from behind. When the Camaro made impact, the pickup swerved across the center lane, nearly hitting an oncoming car. Chino jerked the wheel to the right to stay in their lane. He looked in the mirror.

"Who's that?" asked Ericka.

"A yellow Camaro. Looks like a woman."

"Is it Cocoa?"

"No. I've never seen her."

"Probably another one of your women," Ericka said.

The Camaro slammed into the back of the pickup again and Chino struggled to stay on the road. *"Dammit, Ericka!"* he said, *"I know you're pissed, but this ain't the time!"*

Chino jerked the wheel to the right and the truck veered off the road, over the shoulder, and into the brush. He stopped the truck. *"Stay here!"* he said, jumping out. His gun was up and he was turned towards the Camaro, now stopped behind them. He started shooting.

Ericka heard the gunfire before she looked back to see where the driver was. She peeked over the seat to see her—a tough-looking white chick with cropped blonde hair, hiding behind the open Camaro door. She was exchanging volleys with Chino.

"Come out so I can kill you!" the woman yelled.

Chino answered with a succession of bullets, all burying themselves in the door of the Camaro. Ericka thought maybe Chino had hit her, but the woman popped up and started firing again. She had a .45 in each hand and Ericka thought she looked like a tough bitch.

Ericka slipped out the passenger side, maneuvering low, out of sight. Chino and the woman kept firing. Now at the rear of the truck, Erica peered around to see the woman, but she was ducked down out of sight. Every ten seconds or so, Chino fired again.

Ericka broke into a sprint towards the passenger side of the Camaro, momentarily obscured from both Chino and the woman. Ericka was on the side of the Camaro now, making her way towards its rear. The woman stood and started firing again.

"Today's the day you die!" she screamed.

Ericka made her way around the back of the Camaro, peeking around at the woman, standing and firing, ducking, standing and firing, ducking, and so on. Ericka prepared to leap at her, her muscles tensed. The ice picks were in her hands, and she sprang towards the unsuspecting woman. Ericka was close to her, an ice pick up over her head, when she felt the sharp, searing pain in her left shoulder.

"Unnnngggggg!" cried Ericka as she brought the ice pick swooping down into the woman's

skull. The woman started to turn towards her, but the ice pick was lodged halfway into her head. The woman made a crazy, screeching sound, falling back, sitting for a moment, her pistol firing wildly, and she toppled over. The woman was on the ground now, flopping and convulsing with her eyes rolled back in her head. Ericka stood over her, looking down at her. It was then that she brought the other ice pick down hard into the woman's eye, burying it to the hilt.

Ericka's shoulder hurt like hell. She was still crouched over the woman's body. Chino, confused as to what was happening, hadn't fired in a few seconds. At least Ericka didn't *think* he had. The whole thing had been such a crazed, chaotic moment that she'd lost track.

"Don't shoot, Chino!"

"Ericka?!"

She stood, waving her good arm.

"Is she dead?" asked Chino.

"Either that or she fakes real good."

He made his way towards her. Ericka leaned down to grab the ice picks.

Chino said, "You're bleeding, babe."

"No shit. *You shot me, dummy!"*

THIRTY-TWO

IT WAS NIGHT. Chino and Ericka were driving on gravel in the bullet-riddled Camaro, searching for 2000 Road. Each of them was armed to the teeth. Finding the road would prove to be a tough in the dark, but finally Chino located it. Driving down 2000 Road, which stretched several miles, they moved slowly so they could spot the black Escalades.

"Maybe they left a light on for us," said Ericka.

"Maybe they left milk and cookies out, too."

"Chino?"

"Yeah?"

"If anything happens, I want you to know..."

He turned towards her. "I love you, too. If

things don't work out, I want you to know you were worth the trouble."

He could see her grinning in the dark, illuminated by the light of the the dash. "You bet your ass I was."

"You were," he said. He turned back towards the road. "You *are*."

Finally, Chino spotted the house on his side of the road. He couldn't make out much as it was dark as hell. He thought he saw someone milling around up there, but couldn't be sure. The three Escalades were easy to spot, even in the dark.

"This is it," he said. They kept moving.

"You think they saw us?"

"Cars are gonna drive by sometimes. As long as we keep moving and then stash this somewhere, we'll be fine."

"Should we do this?" asked Ericka. "It's not too late to run. Maybe we could go to Mexico."

"It's too late," he said. "You can stay in the car if you want."

"No, baby. It was just a thought."

"Tell you what: we'll go in here and kill a buncha assholes, and then after that we'll go to Mexico."

"I don't have a passport."

"First let's focus on stayin' alive."

About a quarter mile down the road, Chino

found an entrance to a field. There was a closed gate, and he knew he'd found the perfect place to park the Camaro. He pulled in and shut the car off.

Ericka leaned in, and they kissed. The kiss was filled with both passion and awkwardness, each aware it could be their last. When they finished, they got out, saying nothing. They closed the car doors and started the walk towards the farmhouse. Neither of them said a word until Chino finally said, "It's right up here. Let's hang back, stick close to the fence so we're less likely to be seen."

Ericka nodded, saying nothing.

Chino led, finally reaching an edge of the treeline. He peered out, trying to see the farmhouse. He couldn't see any goons on the outside of the yard, but that didn't mean there weren't any lurking in the shadows. His vision was limited, and he could only see this side of the parked vehicles. Although he couldn't make out much on the other side, there were lights on in the house. The curtains were drawn, but there was light inside.

He started moving, doing sort of a half-run, still semi-crouched, heading towards the SUVs with his two .45s raised and ready. He continued looking around, watching, but saw nothing.

When he got to the side of an Escalade, he stopped and squatted. He turned to look for Ericka and faintly saw her right behind him. She was squatting too.

Chino edged towards the rear of the Escalade and peered towards the front of the house through the space between vehicles. He could see the cherry of a cigarette now and when he squinted, he could see the faint figure of the guy smoking it up there on the porch.

"There's a guy up there," he whispered.

Ericka said nothing. Chino started to move but reconsidered. He turned to ask Ericka if she'd heard him, but she was gone. Suddenly, Chino felt real, intense fear. He felt cold, and his heart started to race. He looked back towards the guard, but he didn't see Ericka. Chino continued creeping towards the back of the second Escalade, planning to make his way towards the porch through the space between the closed garage and the vehicles. Then he would creep up on the man and kill him with his hands so as not to make noise. When he came to the rear of the second Escalade, he looked back but still didn't see his wife.

He turned back towards the house and saw Ericka's figure moving up the walkway from the driveway to the porch. There was no time for

Chino to do anything, and he feared Ericka would be killed. As he watched her, moving half-crouched, Chino saw the man drop his cigarette. Then he saw a blur of motion where Ericka was, and he saw the man make a strange movement. He heard a quiet grunt and then he saw the guard fall over. Chino smiled, realizing Ericka had killed him with one of her knives.

Okay, she'd killed the guard, but she couldn't take them all. And it seemed unlikely the guy she'd killed was Saint Lewis, although he couldn't know for sure. He moved quickly, making his way towards her. When he was six or seven feet behind her, he whispered, *"Ericka."* She turned towards him, her Glock raised.

"It's me," he said. Neither said a word, and she let Chino take the lead again. He was halfway up the porch steps when he turned and said, "Hang back a minute." Ericka stayed on the steps, two from the top, as Chino stood on the porch. He stuck one of his pistols into his waistline to free his hand. He tried the door. The screen door was unlocked. He pulled it open, its creaking quiet enough to not cause alarm. Standing inside the screen, he tried the wooden door. He turned the knob, but it was locked.

He thought about it, wondering if he could bust the door in. It would be a gamble, he thought, and if it didn't break, it could be a costly one. Fuck it, he thought. He knocked on the door. There was a pause and then he heard a voice inside.

"What's up?" asked the voice.

Chino knocked a second time. There was another pause before a gunshot blasted through the door, just missing him. Chino raised his .45 and fired a round through the door, feeling confident he'd struck the man. Chino stepped back and rammed himself into the door with his shoulder, as hard as he could. The door burst open, and Chino sort of stumbled in, his pistol up. The door caught midway on the dead guy. There was another guy, the fucker wearing sunglasses, standing to the right. Chino shot him before he could move, and the guy toppled. Chino pushed his way inside and caught a bullet in his right arm, causing him to drop his pistol. He spun to his right and shot the fucker with the gun with his left hand. Another guy came from an area behind them. Chino swiveled and popped off a shot, striking him.

"Get outta my way!" said Ericka. *"I want some, too!"*

Chino continued moving forward, around a recliner and then to his right, peering back into the room from which the last guy had come. Immediately, another goon popped out, and Chino shot him in the face. Chino looked to his left, seeing an empty kitchen area and a closed back door. He returned to the living room where all the dead guys were. Ericka was standing there with her Glock raised, staring down an empty hallway. Walking down that four-door hallway worried him.

He made his way to the first door, on his left, and used his right hand to open it. It was empty. He sighed out of relief. He then turned towards the door behind him. He opened it carefully, making a point to stand back in case someone started firing. He pushed the door open and found a dark bathroom. He switched on the light, but no one was there.

Now there were just two doors ahead—one on each side, directly across from each other.

He didn't want to do it, but he saw no other way. He turned towards Ericka, right behind him. "I'll take the door on the left. You take the one on the right."

Ericka nodded.

Chino maneuvered himself in front of his door, stopping to allow Ericka to get into position. They were both facing their respective doors, about to go inside, when a gun fired from the open end of the hall. "*Owwww!*" screamed

Chino as the bullet struck the shoulder of his uninjured arm, causing him to drop his gun again. Chino turned to see the big black guy drop his pistol, grabbing at a butterfly knife stuck in his throat. The guy dropped to his knees, his hands clutched at the knife. He looked up, and then finally, he fell face-forward.

Chino looked at Ericka and nodded with a grin.

They both turned back towards their doors. Chino picked up the .45 with his left hand, both arms hurting like a sonofabitch. He opened his door. When he did, Chino saw the big bald fucker standing there with his Sig Sauer aimed at him.

The fucker was grinning, and Chino recognized him.

"I know you."

"And I know you," said Saint Lewis. "You're Chino Genetti."

Chino glared at him. *"You're the fucker who chewed off my ear!"*

Saint Lewis' expression changed. He stared at Chino, tilting his head. "I don't remember you," said Saint Lewis. "But then I've chewed off so many guys' ears." He shrugged, his grin widening.

"Not a day has gone by I haven't thought about you."

"I got you dead to rights. I could kill you as easy as a politician lies. Let's say we just drop the guns and go at this man-to-man and see who's best."

Chino grinned a tired grin. "You mighta noticed, I been shot a couple times."

Saint Lewis nodded. "I did. That's a shame, but we gotta work with what we got."

"Like havin' one ear your whole life."

The bastard smiled. "I suppose so. So what you say? We gonna fight, or am I gonna shoot you down like a dog?"

Chino shrugged, and the pain in his shoulder increased. He dropped his .45.

Saint Lewis, still smiling, said, "I could just shoot you now. Wouldn't that be somethin'?"

"You wouldn't do that," said Chino. "You're a man of honor, even if you are an ear-chewin' piece of shit."

Saint Lewis chuckled, dropping the Sig. He approached Chino. Normally, Chino loved to fight, but this guy had already kicked his ass once and, on top of that, Chino was injured. There was no way this would end well.

Saint Lewis lunged towards him headfirst, shoving him back against the wall. Chino pushed back, getting a weak uppercut in, and they toppled to the floor, wrestling. There was a gunshot in the next room. Chino and Saint Lewis were still rolling around on the floor when Ericka walked in.

"Get back, Chino," she said. "I'll shoot the fucker."

"No!" said Chino. *"He's mine!"*

Ericka shook her head. "Stupid macho bullshit."

Saint Lewis and Chino were locked in each other's arms when Chino reared his head back and slammed it hard into his face. Saint Lewis loosened his grip, and Chino kneed him in the balls. As Saint Lewis recoiled, trying to regain his bearings, Chino pushed himself up slowly. He was almost up when Saint Lewis clocked him in the side of his head, knocking him down again.

"You shoulda took the bullet," Saint Lewis said.

"Fuck you," growled Chino.

Now it was Saint Lewis' turn to headbutt Chino, and the headbutt rocked him. Pain shot through Chino's head and he saw stars. Saint Lewis climbed on top of him. "Say goodbye, fucker," he said, putting his hands over Chino's face. Just as he was about to dig his thumbs into

Chino's eyes, Ericka said, "Goodbye, fucker," and shot him in the back of the head. Saint Lewis fell over. Chino looked up at Ericka.

"Dammit, I had this."

Chino grabbed Saint Lewis' body and pulled his head close to his face.

"What are you doin'?" Ericka asked.

"Settlin' an old score," said Chino. He pulled Saint Lewis' ear to his mouth and bit into it, shaking his head to tear it loose. Once he had, he pushed the guy's body off of him. He looked at Ericka with blood all over his mouth, turning his head to spit out the ear.

"What the hell?" Ericka asked.

"I'll explain later."

"You'd better."

Chino pushed himself up slowly. He was back on his feet, but he was wobbling. He looked at Ericka, wiping the blood off his mouth with his forearm.

"I guess you weren't the best hitman alive after all," she said, grinning.

"Well, I am now."

He picked up his .45 and Saint Lewis' Sig Sauer. He looked at Ericka. "Did you get her?"

"Who? Cocoa?"

"I heard a shot."

"No," she said. "Just some fucker tryin' to rape me."

"I guess this is what life is now," he said. He stepped into the hallway just as a deafening shotgun blast roared from the end of the hall. Chino looked and saw Cocoa holding a pump shotgun. No sooner than this registered, Ericka shot Cocoa in the leg. The shotgun dropped and Cocoa fell to her knees, crying out in pain. Chino fired a shot now, into Cocoa's left arm, and Cocoa fell on her back. He moved closer and fired again, shooting her other arm. She howled with pain.

"Don't kill her," said Ericka.

"I know," said Chino, firing into her other leg.

Cocoa lay there, bleeding and moaning. *"Goddamn you, Chino!"*

Ericka pulled off her backpack and started rummaging through it.

"I don't think you two have met," said Chino.

"We're about to," said Ericka as she pulled out the ice picks.

"What are those for?" asked Cocoa, her eyes huge.

"I brought you some gifts," Ericka said.

"Please, no!"

"I heard you were a fan of ice picks," said Ericka. "So, I stopped and got some, special for you."

Cocoa recoiled, but was unable to move. She was frantic. She looked at Chino with desperate eyes. "It don't have to be this way," she said. "I'll give you money. I got money. There's a duffel bag filled with cash in the back of my Escalade. You let me go, it's yours."

"Fuck your money," Chino said.

"Then what?"

"We want two things," said Ericka.

Cocoa stared at her as she wept.

"First, I want you to apologize."

Cocoa stared at her, terrified. "I'm sorry. I really am."

"Not me," said Ericka. "You owe Chino an apology, you nasty bitch."

Cocoa looked at Chino. "Please, Chino. I'm sorry. I'm so fuckin' sorry for all this. Please don't let her do this."

"I said there were two things I wanted," said Ericka.

"What's the other?" asked Cocoa.

"I want you to bleed."

She moved towards Cocoa, an ice pick in each hand. Cocoa's eyes were wide and she begged. "Please no," she said. "From one woman to another."

Ericka crouched down over her, grinning. Cocoa covered her eyes with her hands. Ericka raised one of the ice picks into the air, bringing it down hard through Cocoa's hand and into her eye. *"That's for my daddy!"* screamed Ericka. Cocoa started thrashing around crazily, both hands reaching for the ice pick. Now the other eye was uncovered. Ericka raised the second ice pick, bringing it down hard, deep into Cocoa's eye. *"And this is for tryin' to kill me!"*

Cocoa was still thrashing around, not quite dead yet, when Chino said, "Step aside."

Ericka moved, seeing Chino standing there with the pump shotgun now. Chino racked the shotgun and pointed it at Cocoa.

"This is for Dobbs," he said.

He pulled the trigger, and the shotgun blasted, demolishing Cocoa's head. There was a hole in the floor and blood, brains, and skull everywhere.

Chino dropped the shotgun.

Ericka helped Chino walk, and they made their way to the front door. They stepped over a body and out into the cool night air.

"You still got them smokes?" asked Chino.

"You don't smoke."

"Neither do you."

"Touche'," she said, digging the cigarettes out

of her pocket. The two of them sat on the porch next to the dead guard. Ericka produced a lighter and lit their cigarettes. They sat, holding one another and smoking. A few minutes later, they heard sirens in the distance.

Chino grinned a tired grin. "Mexico woulda been nice," he said.

"So, we goin' to jail?" asked Ericka.

"I don't do jail."

"I guess I should go back inside and get the guns."

She stood.

He looked up. "You forgot somethin'."

She smiled and leaned down, kissing him.

Dear reader,

We hope you enjoyed reading *Let It Kill You*. Please take a moment to leave a review, even if it's a short one. Your opinion is important to us.

Discover more books by Andy Rausch at

https://www.nextchapter.pub/authors/andy-rausch

Want to know when one of our books is free or discounted? Join the newsletter at

http://eepurl.com/bqqB3H

Best regards,

Andy Rausch and the Next Chapter Team

You might also like:
The Suicide Game by Andy Rausch

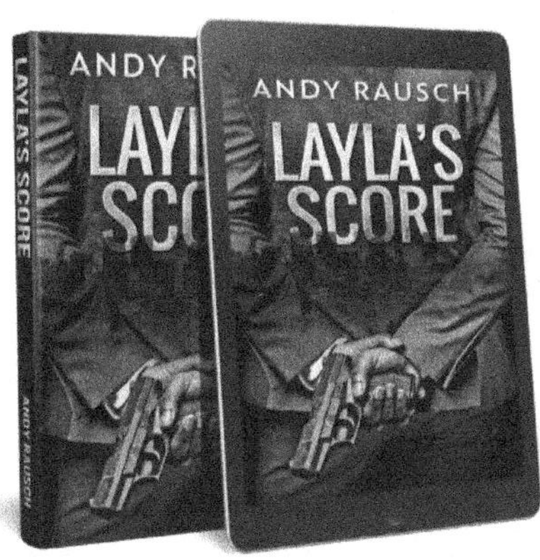

To read the first chapter for free, head to:
https://www.nextchapter.pub/books/laylas-score

CPSIA information can be obtained
at www.ICGtesting.com
Printed in the USA
BVHW071353250521
608094BV00002B/122